The Gretchen Question

Also by Jessica Treadway

The Gretchen Question

a novel by

Jessica Treadway

Delphinium Books

THE GRETCHEN QUESTION

For information, address DELPHINIUM BOOKS, INC.,
16350 Ventura Boulevard, Suite D
PO Box 803
Encino, CA 91436

Library of Congress Cataloging-in-Publication Data is available
on request.
ISBN 978-1-883285-89-0
20 21 22 LSC 10 9 8 7 6 5 4 3 2 1

First Edition

To Cassis and August Henry, with thanks and love–
past, present, future

She always had the feeling that it was very, very dangerous to live even one day.

–Virginia Woolf, *Mrs. Dalloway*

It was the simplest of tasks that lay before me: I was to move the bins.

I looked forward to the pleasure of doing this favor for my friend. After my work meeting at the hospital, I would drive to Grettie's house instead of my own. How many times have I made the trip between us? Too many to guess at. How many *more* times will I make it—that's the question.

It's the solstice, the third week of June. The cusp of summer just outside Boston: impossible to overstate how pretty it is here, how filled with greenness and hope. When I saw the peacefulness of the morning, its beauty, my heart rose and wanted to stay there. But beneath the pleasure I anticipated, I felt nervous.

It wasn't just me. All the towns around here were nervous. On edge. That was far as you could go—you couldn't say panicked or petrified. Nobody had gotten hurt. Nothing had been stolen except food. Someone was breaking into houses while people were away—for the day, for the weekend—and spending time in the family rooms. The owners would come home and find a blanket they'd left draped over the sofa lying rumpled across the cushions, as if someone had lain beneath it, then cast the throw aside. TV channels had been changed, the remote control in a place other than where the owners had left it. People started referring to the intruder as "the

Snack Burglar," and I guess to show that they were serious about catching him, the police went so far as to take fingerprints from the TV remotes and test them against what they had in their database. No match. No idea who was doing it. "A disturbed individual," the police chief said in an interview on the local news.

"We urge everyone in the community to be vigilant," he added. "I know there's a nickname floating around out there, that might lead some people to take this more lightly than they should. Criminals often start small and progress to bigger actions. Just because the situation might seem relatively harmless now doesn't mean it will stay that way."

A sample item in the published police log looked like this:

> Officers responded to a call from a Birch Road address when the residents returned home from school and work to find that their home had been entered in their absence. The intruder had apparently watched television and eaten a sleeve of Ritz crackers and a container of leftover take-out food. Police have no leads at this time. The residents were advised to lock their doors from now on.

They hadn't locked their doors! I'm ashamed to say that when I read that, my sympathies shifted from the victims to what I know from crime shows is called the "perpetrator." I know that an unlocked door is not the same thing as an invitation to enter. But I pictured the intruder, the perpetrator, merely looking for a place to rest, and something to eat. It would probably turn out to be a homeless or mentally ill person who could have stolen jewelry or something else to sell, but didn't. Who would only go so far and not compromise his integrity. That was something in his favor, I thought.

Also, who keeps such track of their crackers that they know when a sleeve is missing, for God's sake?

I always lock my door. I keep it locked even when I am inside.

The first thing I did was check the weather forecast online. It's been hot all week, and the temp was again headed upwards of eighty degrees, so I was a little worried—I used to do just fine in the heat, but lately, not so much. When I took Scout out for his early walk, the sun already warmed the top of my head like the palm of a gentle and giant hand. Afterward, I finally allowed myself to dig out my warm-weather clothes. I'd been superstitious about it, afraid to trust I'd see summer, but now here it was.

It would be a full day, what with my work meeting, the favor for Grettie, and the appointment with the therapist at three o'clock. There was a time in my life, especially when my son was young, that every day was a full day, but lately they've been pretty light. I knew it was a good idea to pace myself. I'd better take things slow.

First the work meeting, then the bins. Then. . .

But I didn't need to worry about that now. I was determined to delay feeling anxious about it until two hours before we were to meet. The therapist had once advised me to schedule "worry time," during which I was allowed to think as much as I wanted about whatever agitated me. These thoughts could include all the what-ifs and fantasies my mind could conjure (no matter how outrageous), but aside from that specified block of minutes or hours, I must do my best to reject any worries that sneaked in.

I was skeptical, I admit. But I also have to admit that it worked, at least a little.

For instance, it helped me sleep on the night before my surgery two years ago. As I lay in the dark I told myself that when morning came, I could let my fear run away with itself, but not before then. The technique isn't perfect by any means, but sometimes it works well enough to keep me from fretting all day about an afternoon appointment, like the one I had later. I would allow myself to begin fretting at one o'clock.

As for the bins, Jack had planned a trip for his and Grettie's twenty-fifth wedding anniversary without taking into account that they'd miss the trash and recycling day for their street. Their town ordinances dictated that they couldn't leave empty receptacles in front of the house for more than a few days. But neither did they want to leave a full garbage barrel in the sealed garage for another week.

A year ago, they could have just asked one of their neighbors to help out. But now, since they're at odds with most of the people on their street, Grettie asked me to swing by and move the containers from the curb into the backyard.

It's not far for me; their town is right next to mine and only a fifteen-minute drive when it isn't rush hour, and she knows I have flexibility during my day. But she still hesitated to request the favor, I could tell. She felt bad about taking the trip at all, right now, even though she didn't know how far away they'd be because Jack had not told her: it was a "surprise destination" anniversary trip. "Are you sure you're up for it?" she asked me before they left. "You know how fast a week goes, right? We'll be back in no time. You'll be fine."

I couldn't help realizing that it would have been more than twenty-five years—nearly thirty!—if it had been Grettie and me celebrating the length of our lives together. And I tried hard, as I always did, not to resent Jack for taking her away at a time when I might really need her. I always suspected him of being at least a little jealous of my friendship with Grettie, even though she told me No, he didn't feel that way at all.

But never mind, I told myself. Never mind, as I have told myself so often during these years.

The trash and recycle trucks made separate trips to the street but both routes were always finished by mid-day, Grettie told me. My work meeting was scheduled for noon. At ten, I clicked into the file I'd moved to the head of my queue in the hospital database, figuring that I would likely be finished within an hour. It was a case of the flu complicated by irregularities in the patient's heart.

PATIENT ID: 1998207
DIAGNOSIS: Influenza, cardiac arrhythmia, atrial fibrillation
INDICATIONS: The patient is a 47-year-old woman of average weight and otherwise good health who reports having suffered from flu symptoms

(head and muscle ache, fever, congestion) two weeks earlier, self-treated with acetaminophen (Tylenol brand) and OTC cough medication. She reports the symptoms abated, then returned along with dizziness, shortness of breath, and confusion. Examination indicates tachycardia and atrial fibrillation.

RELEVANT HISTORY: The patient acknowledges use of cocaine over a period of about three months in her mid-20s. She reports that she experienced occasional symptoms of tachycardia during that time, but did not seek medical attention.

DISPOSITION: Patient was admitted for overnight monitoring and observation.

When arrhythmia continued, and in light of other symptoms indicating stroke risk, ablation surgery was scheduled. Patient signed consent.

PROCEDURE: The patient was brought into the operating room and placed in the supine position on the operating table. An intravenous line was started, and sedation anesthesia was administered IV. The patient was monitored for cardiac rate, blood pressure, and oxygen saturation continuously.

After 10-15 minutes several incisions were made in the chest and ultrasound energy was applied to create scar tissue in the heart to block abnormal electrical signals causing arrhythmia. Measurements were taken to ensure that the scar tissue now directed electrical signals through a controlled path to the lower heart chambers. Incision was closed and dressed. The procedure was completed without complication and tolerated well.

FOLLOW-UP CARE: Patient was moved to ICU for observation and monitoring. Diuretics and anti-coagulants were prescribed. Patient was up and walking one day after surgery, discharged to home with instructions to continue diuretics for two weeks. Follow-up scheduled in a month.

I knew this patient. Well, not knew personally (if I'd known her, I would have had to send the file to someone else), but remembered, from other case notes I had coded over the years. Her patient ID had caught my eye at first because 1998 was the year my son was born, and 207 had been the number of the triple-decker I lived in, on the outskirts of the city, when I gave birth to him. But over time, I had other reasons to pay attention to this patient's file. We were the same age. The first time I coded her, she'd been treated for a septate uterus, which led to a miscarriage. I remember how sad I felt, reading this; my own son was two years old at the time. Since then, she had been treated for a nasal deformity (minor); appendicitis (more cause for concern, but caught in time); a successful pregnancy six years ago (I was so happy for her, to see that news!); and now this, the most serious of all.

What had she been confused about when she came in with symptoms? And why had she done cocaine in her twenties, and what had stopped her after three months? I imagined a boyfriend who was what my mother would have called "a bad influence"; I imagined her coming to her senses, knowing that she had to leave him, fearing his reaction both because he was on drugs and because he did not want to lose her. I imagined the talk she'd had with herself and the decision she knew she must make: stay with this loser and lose myself in the process, or make a clean break, from him and his way of life. Of course, this was all a complete fantasy on my part. It was just as likely that she'd tried cocaine at a party, liked it, and would never have stopped using if her parents or a friend hadn't intervened and forced her to get help. But I liked to tell myself stories about the patients I coded. It appealed to the English major in me.

The patient's name was Celia Santoro. I was not supposed to know it, but—through no fault of my own—I did. I also knew that the procedure she had undergone, ablation, was called a "heart maze." It had been performed a month and a half earlier; was she all right now? Once I learned her name, I couldn't help (or *didn't* help, take your pick) looking up where she lived. Her address was in the town just east of mine, probably ten miles away from where I sat at my desk coding her medical file. Sometimes I was almost tempted to drive by her house, to see if I might catch a glimpse of her—to see if she looked anything like what I imagined.

But of course, I would not. It would violate the ethics of my profession.

"How can that possibly not be the most boring job in the world?" my son asked me once, when he was in fifth grade. "You sit at a desk and read about the boring medical procedures people had done to them. Then you sit in a basement and compare notes with people who do the same boring thing. You turn people into numbers, and for what? Insurance companies. How can that feed your soul?"

He didn't mean to be obnoxious, I told myself. It scared me, I admit, to hear that tone in his voice—I'd heard it before, I'd seen that look. But I convinced myself that it wasn't the same tone or the same look; he was genuinely curious, he genuinely wanted to know. He must have heard someone use that phrase, "feed your soul," in a sincere way—it's the way people talk around here. When I was young it was *Follow your dream.*

I bit back the impulse to inform him that it didn't feed my soul. But it fed him. Kept him in this house in this town with its school district that might not be as fancy as the one Grettie's kids went to, but was still pretty damn good. And in the clothes he liked to wear, the music he liked to listen to, and the games he liked to play. All those tai chi lessons! Now, it pays for his college—or some of it, the portion not paid for by the loans he's taken out, which I try not to think about.

My salary alone wouldn't have been enough. I make thirty dollars an hour as a medical coder, and that's now, after almost twenty years. I still think it's better than anything I could have gotten with my degree in English, which is why I took the job in the first place. Coding was fairly new then, it was easy to stay employed. Property taxes alone eat up about a fifth of my annual earnings. Until this spring, I supplemented my salary by teaching a night class in coding certification at the community college. I can't imagine what Will thinks I must be paid for my work. If he's ever bothered to wonder, he's never asked.

But that's kind of how it is, here. Ours used to be more of a blue-collar town, but then in came the bike path and now it's literally an extension of Cambridge. Most kids are accustomed to their parents having enough money for whatever they want. I guess it's not Will's fault, those things he said to me.

I told him: "I know it isn't your idea of exciting. But somebody has to code those doctors' notes." I knew he would not understand it if I said what I really thought, which was that I thought of each file as a story. And that what I did for a living is the same thing we all do, all the time. When it comes down to it, anything one person ever says to another can be construed as code. "It's the way the system works," I said instead. When he smirked, my heart sank, but I kept trying. "I think of it as a kind of translation. From one language into another."

At this he laughed outright. "Yeah, right. It's pure poetry."

Well, there was no way I could turn this into anything else in my head—the meanness, the disrespect. "I'm not saying it's poetry." If someone had told me what it could be like to be the single mother of a single son, I might never have had him. This was what I told myself some-times—that it was because I was doing it all alone, be-cause I had no siblings to offer him—to avoid believing it was my fault, the way Will acted and the things he said to me.

But we got through it, thank God. He started taking tai chi classes in middle school, and they seemed to make him a little calmer, less likely to pester me about who his father was or anything else. Soon after that the emeto-phobia set in, though we didn't call it that—we called it the trouble with his tummy—and we stopped arguing altogether, probably because he couldn't afford for us to be fighting when he had that going on. He was vulnerable, he needed me. He became my sweet boy again, right up until he left for college last August. When we had the worst fight of all.

He's not a bad person—of course he isn't! Or a mean person, or an unfeeling one. (Look at all the feelings he has for his girlfriend.) He's just somebody who needs to recognize that he's allowed his priorities to get out of whack. Isn't it more important to keep loving the parent you know than to agonize about the parent you don't? But try telling him that.

After I finished coding and submitting Celia's file, I logged out of the system and shut the computer down altogether. As I reached for the switch, there came a memory I wasn't sure I wanted. Was it the sight of my own arm, sleeveless because of the hot day? How Will, when he was little, would rub my bare arm up and down the way other children would rub a blankie. He'd do it in bed after his bath, when I picked him up from preschool, and whenever he felt nervous. I remember longing for it, the arm-rubbing, even as it was happening.

How is it possible to miss a thing before you've lost it? And yet, I did. We do.

After I logged out of my work program, I took Scout for another short walk around the block. He's almost ten now; we've had him since Will was in fourth grade, when he asked if we could get a dog. It wasn't my idea, I didn't want one. Well, that's not exactly true. I was happy to have a dog, I just also dreaded it because I knew what always follows having a dog, the dog has to die. I didn't want Will to have to go through that. To be honest, I didn't want to go through it, myself.

He started bringing up the idea after we went with Grettie and her son Cam to one of the Harvard museums, where we saw a sculpture of a robed, reclining corpse with a dog at his feet. *Fidelity beyond the grave*, read the exhibit plaque, so I explained to Will what "fidelity" meant. I could tell that of all the art we saw during that visit, this piece affected him the most. "If you lie down or if you die," he said to me solemnly the next day, "a dog will keep you company forever. Don't you think that would be nice?"

Not for that reason but because he wanted it so much I let myself be persuaded, and as it turned out, Scout became more of a companion to me than to Will, because he was at school all day and I was working at home. He was a beagle mix from the pound, nothing special. They didn't charge us anything, we just went over one day and brought him home. Will said he liked having another boy in the house, which I thought was adorable. When he took up tai chi, Scout took to lying across the room and watching. Will said Scout's eyes followed his every move. He said he thought it settled them both down—the dog, and him. I thought that was adorable, too.

When Scout and I got back from the walk I poured some food into his bowl, then considered putting on the exercise video the surgeon's nurse recommended after my surgery, to help me recover. I was compliant back then, and did it every day. But for the past few weeks—who am I kidding, for the past few months now—I haven't been able to summon the energy, or the motivation. My heart's felt too low in my chest. I decided I would just eat a little breakfast and then set out, first to my work meeting and then to perform my chore. There was no need, of course, for the trash and garbage receptacles to be replaced so soon after they had been emptied, but it is in my nature to avoid procrastinating; procrastinating makes me nervous.

Besides, it made sense to carry out the errand at Grettie and Jack's on the way to my appointment with the therapist, rather than the other way around. I had no way of knowing what I would feel like when I left the therapist's office.

I took a shower and tried on a couple of different outfits in front of the mirror. Finally I chose a tunic with bright colors, hoping the pattern and the loose fit would distract people from looking too closely at my arms or my face, which I guess have gotten too thin now for me to camouflage. Funny—I remember buying the blouse, a few years ago, in the hope that it would cover my extra pounds. Now I hoped it would cover the fact that I've lost more than I can afford. Not that I actually notice this myself, but Grettie's mentioned it enough times, and if I'm honest, I have to say I've also seen it in the way other people look at me.

I went to the kitchen to let my hair dry as I stood at the sink, eating a slice of leftover frozen pizza. I had long hair before, but it's short now, and I love the convenience of not having to blow it dry.

I used to fix myself a proper breakfast every day, and I still do, sometimes. Oatmeal, scrambled eggs, or fruit and toast. But sometimes, now, I either skip it or eat whatever's closest at hand. If I'm tired and I want leftover pizza for breakfast, then that's what I eat.

My kitchen window looks out onto the yard my apartment building shares with three others. The townhouses are kind of like small dorms on the four corners of a rectangular quad. From my window I can look into the kitchen twenty or so yards across from me, and see Pascal. I used to try to catch her eye, but I don't anymore, because at some point it became clear to me that she was trying not to notice me doing it. It made me sad, but it couldn't be helped. There are times I want to call her up, or go over, and say Pascal, this is so silly. We live close enough to toss a package of spaghetti between our windows (we actually did that once, a long time ago, when her water was already boiling before she realized she had no pasta to put in it), and here we haven't spoken about anything substantive, anything personal, in so many years.

As I stood eating my cold pizza, I saw her washing dishes at her sink. A cloud passed fast over the quad, and we both looked up at the sudden sight of the sun. When our eyes met, I waved as I used to do all the time. She appeared to hesitate for a moment, then waved back. She didn't return my smile, but she did raise a hand.

The elation this created in me was far out of proportion to what the gesture warranted. Wasn't it? Yet who was to say, really? If I was happy to have my old friend acknowledge me after so much time, wasn't it my right to feel that way?

Then she stepped away from the window, and the cloud blocked the sun again. I washed down the last bite of pizza with some flat Diet Coke, then set out for the drive twelve miles north to the hospital.

But my car wouldn't start. This happened every so often, but when I took it into the shop, the mechanics said they didn't see anything that might account for it. I had them replace the battery last time, in case, and it seemed fine for a while, until now.

Eight tries before the engine turned over. Another sort of person might have taken it as an omen about the trip she was embarking upon. But I am not that sort of person. I backed out carefully and drove down my street on the lookout for cats or other animals, which sometimes dart across without looking. Stupid. I hit a squirrel once, but never a cat. I'm afraid I will, though, so I always drive very slowly until I get to the end of the road.

At the highway, it wasn't until I was about to turn onto the ramp that I saw it was closed off by three orange traffic cones, and a sign instructing me to *Seek Alternate Route.* No indication as to why the sign was there—no men in hardhats, no trucks or emergency vehicles, nothing I could see that was blocking or contaminating the road—just the sign and the cones placed exactly so as to prevent me from proceeding where I wanted to go. I drove past the blockade, now headed in the wrong direction and feeling suddenly, absurdly, that I might cry.

Knowing that I needed to put the address of the hospital into my phone's GPS and find a back route, I pulled into the parking lot of Apex, the athletic club I'd belonged to for a few years when Grettie gave me a membership as a Christmas gift, before Will took tennis lessons there. Every Monday at lunchtime, I went to a yoga class taught by a middle-aged, bulky black woman who didn't seem to mind teaching a gym filled with only white people. The class always left me in a good mood. I liked how she ended every class while we were lying in the corpse pose. "You stand in the center of your own inner peace," she'd say in this calm kind of singsong, and I tried to believe this. Usually believing it only lasted as long as the class did, but that was better than not believing it at all.

But then one day I threw my back out trying to achieve a pose, and didn't return even after my back got better, afraid of repeating the injury. It turned out, I heard later, that the yoga teacher had been fired for not being a yoga teacher at all, but some imposter who enjoyed watching us smug middle-aged suburbanites twist ourselves into painful and unhealthy positions while she gave increasingly complex instructions from her mat at the front of the

room. "Now thread your left arm under your right knee–
balance on two toes of each foot–inhale to a count of six-
teen and exhale to a count of thirty-two." Turned out, she
made all those "poses" up. No wonder my back hurt–what
kind of person did something like that? And yet I had liked
her. The gym's manager told me, when I inquired, that
Apex had a zero-tolerance policy when it came to things
like what the "yoga teacher" had been fired for.

That was a pretty good trick she'd played on us, I had
to admit. I felt hurt, though, because I'd liked the teacher,
and I'd felt vulnerable in her class, trying to make my body
do all those things she'd convinced us were good for it.

If some of the people in the class had not felt so embarrassed by how she had humiliated them, they might have
started a petition requesting that she be given a second
chance. It's the kind of thing people who live around here
do. But she had humiliated them, so they did not.

It's not really the reason I left that yoga class, because
I threw my back out. No, the real reason is that one time
when I was lying there at the end of the hour, listening to
the "teacher" say those words about standing in the center
of my own inner peace, I turned my head and happened
to see the woman on the mat next to mine, lying the same
way I was. The way we all were–like, well, corpses. I knew
it was only a pose, but I'd never seen it from the outside
before.

The woman, who was only a little older than me,
looked for all the world as if she were dead. I knew she was
not dead, only relaxed, but knowing it didn't make any
difference–it freaked me out so much that I couldn't go

back, to that class or any other. By the time I even thought about trying it again, the imposter had been found out and ejected. There was some talk of pressing charges, but I never heard any follow-up.

This morning, despite the fact that I felt an urgency to make up some time, I got out of my car in the gym's parking lot and leaned against it, taking in some air. I felt a little faint—the sun was so hot—but I've developed strategies for when this happens, like closing my eyes for a few moments or putting water on my face. I didn't have any water with me, but I tried closing my eyes. When I opened them I saw a man coming out of Apex and looking my way, and before I could avoid his gaze, I realized that we knew each other. Though he was older and heavier now, I remembered him as the tennis pro who'd taught the lessons Will took with some other kids back when they were in middle school, after I'd quit the gym myself.

The lessons had been Trudy Foote's idea. She'd signed her son Derek up, and she wanted him to have a pal or two in the class. I couldn't afford it, but Grettie paid for her own son and mine. Maybe one or both of them would take to it, she said, and end up getting a tennis scholarship someday. This was what persuaded me, along with the fact that I knew she wasn't going to tell Jack that she was paying for Will's lessons as well as Cam's. I know I should be ashamed to admit it, but I loved our having a secret from Jack, even such a small one.

"Hi!" the pro said, recognizing me. "It's Roberta, right? Mrs. Chase?" I'd never told him it wasn't *Mrs.*— what business was it of his? He took a step closer. "Hey, you okay? Should I go get somebody? Or call inside?"

Shit! So much for hiding what I didn't want anyone to see. But I would do my best to pretend I didn't know why he was asking me these things. "No, thanks," I told him. "I'm on my way to work, I'm just taking a little break."

He said "Okay" in a weird tone, but then I remembered that he'd always been weird. When he added, "So how's our boy doing?" I knew he had forgotten my son's name. Which was all right, because I'd forgotten his. I answered "Fine," without giving him the satisfaction of reminding him it was *Will.* "What's he up to now?" the pro asked, and I told him where Will went to college.

"He's studying psychology and biology," I added. "He might do premed." Will had not exactly told me this, it was just something I thought might happen.

"Wow. Smart kid." The tennis pro seemed uncomfortable, standing there having a conversation with me, but he kept up his end of the small talk. He asked if "our boy" had kept up with the game. I told him No, he didn't play tennis anymore, he was pretty heavily into tai chi.

The tennis pro didn't seem to know what to say to that. He adjusted the load of his bag from one shoulder to the other and said, "Hey, would you be willing to write me a recommendation? Or a testimonial, I guess it would be called. For my website. I'm thinking about going totally private, this place is for the birds." He jerked his thumb backward at the Apex sign behind him. The club's logo was a jagged line aspiring toward the top of a graph. "They pay crap, and if I have to pretend I give a shit about whether one more middle-aged woman can add some pop to her serve, I might just collapse on the court and die." He smiled as if of course I could understand his plight.

I made a murmuring sound which, I knew, could have been taken to mean anything. I've been making the same sound all my life, on the many occasions upon which I feel expected to offer an opinion but do not feel prepared.

Then I said, "Okay" to his testimonial question. I was confident I would not have to follow through, because he wouldn't be able to track me down when I didn't supply what he wanted.

"You sure you'd be up to it?" he asked. "I don't want to—"

"Of course," I interrupted him, irritated. "You have a card or something?"

Once, Will told me that Derek Foote had puked on the court when this pro made them do suicide drills and refused to let Derek stop because he had a stitch in his side. "Are you an athlete or a pussy?" the pro had asked, and when Derek threw up, the pro turned away in disgust and said he guessed he had his answer.

He dropped the tennis bag now and rummaged loudly through one of its compartments, then swore when the search did not yield the business card he was looking for. "Tell you what—you could just drop it off at the desk in there," he told me. "In a sealed envelope, okay? I don't trust any of those schmoes."

I told him Okay again and he said it was great to see me, and that I should take care, and I said *You, too,* before we parted. I am sure we both understood that I was not going to write the note he had asked for on his behalf. I hoped he did not also understand—or did I hope the oppo-site?—how much satisfaction this gave me.

I got in my car, but had trouble starting it again. Six tries, this time, before I could pull out. The pro had parked on the far side of the lot, so we reached the exit simulta-neously. Someone had to give. He smiled and waved me on, and I proceeded before him, but wait! *Was* it a smile and a wave? As I passed by, assuming that he was smiling and waving, it seemed that what I might actually be seeing was a sneer and the finger! Could he possibly have been giving me the finger? I gasped as I turned back onto the main road, and behind me he sounded his horn. Friendly good-bye tap, or a blast saying *Fuck you, you bitch?* The idea that it might have been this second thing struck me like a slap, even though I'd been the one with the intention of slighting him.

I was still only a mile away from my own house. All I really wanted now was to return home, stretch out on the wicker chaise on the screened porch, and alternately doze and read. I'm enjoying, so much, my current book—I have not read Virginia Woolf before (as an English major, it shames me to admit), and though I find that I need to read certain sentences more than once, I end up every time be-ing glad I did.

Oh if she could have had her life over again! If I were a person who underlined, that sentence I would have lit up in yellow. *The agony was so terrific.* It's after reading lines like these that I have to set the novel aside. Reading it takes longer than reading a simpler book, but how long it takes isn't everything.

I was tempted to call in sick to my meeting and return home to pick up the novel, but no. I would have my time, soon, to rest and read. Such moments of luxury have to be paid for, and first I would go to my work meeting, then move the bins. After that, my appointment with the therapist. Checking the clock in my car, I saw with some relief that I still had a good deal of time before the hour I'd designated to begin worrying.

The chaise, though: it held onto my imagination. There was a time in my life when I was afraid to lie down, because it was while I was in this position–let's face it, in the corpse pose–that I felt the full measure of my despair. In the years after I followed Grettie to Boston, before Will was born, I thought about killing myself. On my bathroom mirror I taped a yellow sticky note containing the final line of a poem I'd read once, and loved. "God does not leave us comfortless, so let evening come." Even if I hadn't been an English major I would have understood that evening meant death, and I left the line where I could see it when I needed to believe that ending it all was an option.

My sister and I didn't grow up going to church, but I've never had the usual trouble believing there's a God. In fact, it seems kind of arrogant to me, the disdain people show for the idea. As if they're afraid to acknowledge that there might be something more or better than what they know–or *think* they know–to exist on the hard dirt of earth. But why? My only struggle with it lies in trying to catch myself when the vision I conjure is that of a man with a beard and a white robe, looking down at us from the sky.

I know this image comes from all the illustrations I've ever seen of Jesus. As an adult I've tried to let go of this conception, and put another in its place. God as a spirit, invisible but everywhere. God as perpetual witness. God as love.

I don't think God designs or manipulates things, like an architect or a puppeteer. When I imagined killing myself, I didn't consider it an affront to destiny or to some master plan. No—my God would not lay blame or shame on my forehead in receiving me back to the fold. *I know*, He'd say, in whatever language He used to communicate (and is it possible to begin learning that language while we're still alive?). *I know. You tried. It's not for everyone.*

One very cold night—amazing to think it was almost twenty years ago—I went so far as to go to the cemetery near my apartment at the edge of the city and lie down under a bush. I brushed some snow away and made a space to lie in. In retrospect it doesn't make sense for me to have brushed the snow—what difference would it have made, if I actually expected to die? I couldn't have said if it was a real suicide attempt or just the wish not to feel what I felt. The police came before I could fall asleep. I never knew whether they'd just been patrolling the cemetery, or someone saw me and called them. The cops wouldn't say, only made me get into the police car and drove me to the hospital, where I had to stay for three days because it's the law in this state when you pose a danger to yourself.

Only in the hospital did I realize that if I died, it would be Grettie who'd have to clean out my apartment. There was nobody else; my sister lives too far away, and it wasn't the kind of thing she'd be good at handling.

It would have been too much to ask of my best friend. And it would devastate her—wouldn't it? The idea that it might *not* devastate her was one I couldn't allow myself to consider.

If nobody's going to be devastated when you die, then what's the point? Not of dying—of life.

So I never told Grettie about that night, she never even knew I'd been in the hospital.

After that, I did my best to get better. I saw the therapist, which helped, for a while. I had someone to talk to, I believed he cared about me. Then I had my son and I could take the poem down. I stopped thinking about dying. And now, here we are.

The back route from my house to the hospital turned out to be easy, though it took longer than my usual one. As I approached the light near the entrance, a line of big-headed children in wheelchairs was being pushed across the street. It took them longer than the light lasted, and when the horns started up behind me, I was shocked to see a few tears fall onto my lap.

Once, my family was stuck in our car on the George Washington Bridge. We were driving from Worcester to New York so my mother could ask her aunt for money; my sister and I weren't supposed to know that, but we did. It was February, very cold, with snow spitting on the windshield, and traffic was standing still. My father was smoking with the windows closed, and it was all Steph and I could do to hold back coughing, but we managed because it would have made our father mad. I was also wondering what would happen if I had to pee, and for a few minutes the wondering about it made me have to clench my legs, until I saw the dog and the woman and forgot what my body felt.

The woman was holding the dog, which was brown and shivering, as she stood in the middle of the bridge next to a little Fiesta with its emergency blinkers on. We watched, waiting for her to cross the halted traffic to the other side, but she didn't move from where she just stood in the snow swirls, stroking the dog's small ears.

"We couldn't fit her in," my mother said, as if answering a question my sister or I had asked. "We don't have enough room." It would have been easy enough for that small woman and her dog to slide in next to my sister and me on the back seat, but neither of us pointed this out.

"A funny thing about Beetles," our father added after a few more minutes, reaching for his pack of Pall Malls on the dash. "Their engines are in the trunk."

I waited for someone in another car to get out and tell the woman she could sit inside until the snow let up or the traffic jam was over, but nobody did. Ahead of us, all I could see was the stretch of fenders all pointing toward the same place; I could not tell where it ended—or was it where it began? The woman put her nose close to the dog's neck and held him tighter, and I saw the dog squirm and hoped the woman couldn't tell he was trying to escape.

Why wasn't she moving? Why didn't anyone at least roll down a window to talk to her, to see if she was all right? To ask if they should call somebody for her once they made it over the bridge?

But I didn't really want to know the answer, so I

closed my eyes. When finally I felt the car begin to move, I opened my eyes again and watched my father steer straight ahead, never turning to look at where the woman stood inches away from his window, until we had passed her, and then through the back windshield I watched until we were far away from where we'd been stuck, and the dog and the woman were lost through the fogged-in glass. My sister mumbled, "That wasn't nice." But it wasn't clear if our parents heard her, or, really, what she meant, or even whom she was speaking to.

On my way to the hospital the honking around me had ceased, because the kids in wheelchairs were finally out of the way. I passed through the light and into the lot, glancing at the marquee board outside the Methodist Church across the street. *Don't be afraid that your life will end. Be afraid that it will never begin.* It took me a surprisingly long time to read the message, as if it were in a foreign language I'd understood when I was a child, but then forgot.

We meet once a month for a working lunch—Lily, Susannah, Dee, and I—in the basement conference room of the hospital that employs us to do its medical coding. De Coder Ring, Dee calls us. I almost hesitate to confess that, it's so corny, but on the other hand I love being part of this group; we've been working together for fifteen years now and we're not just colleagues, we're friends. Susannah and Dee and I all work from home, so the meetings are our only chance to see each other in person, since we don't get together very often outside of work.

Lily's our team manager, and she schedules the meetings so we can go over new procedures or protocols, and also do postmortems on any problems or mistakes that come up between sessions. After the work part, we talk about what's going on in our lives. One of us asks for advice and the others give it, one of us tells a story about a kid or a bad date or a parent's illness, and the others respond to that, too.

Sometimes one of us is feeling vicarious trauma over a certain file; we get to know these patients, even if it is only by their ID numbers, and over the years we've followed certain ones through different procedures we can't help having feelings about: fertility treatments, miscarriages, cancer surgery, end-of-life care. We get attached to them. We feel invested in their stories, we want them to survive. For me, that patient is 1998207–Celia Santoro. But as coders, of course, we never get to meet them the way their doctors and nurses do, we never get to say how sorry we are when things don't work out. So the four of us talk about that, too.

When I got to the hospital, I took a parking spot and then noticed Dee pulling in right across from me. I could have sworn she saw me in her rearview, and I waved, but she didn't respond. Well, she's the spacey one out of all of us; sometimes she's preoccupied by thinking about her five kids–five kids! I could never do it, but she has a husband to help–and I figured that's what was happening when she stayed in her car, with her phone at her ear. I waited for her to finish talking so we could walk in together, but it was obviously a long call, I didn't want to interrupt or distract her by hanging around, so I headed toward the entrance alone.

There were two young women nurses walking shoulder to shoulder toward me, on their way to the lot. They were dressed in identical smocks, decorated with brightly colored birds–toucans, maybe, or parrots–which made me think they might work in pediatrics. Were the women lovers? I wondered. Then I wondered, What makes me think that? Just because they wore matching smocks, that didn't mean anything. But no, it was something else, something about the way they leaned toward each other as they spoke and didn't seem to see me until I was right next to them. Right before they noticed me, I heard one of them say to the other, "I wish I had it in me to break his heart again." Okay, so they probably weren't lovers.

It was a different kind of intimacy, then.

Suddenly, the pavement shimmered in front of me and I had to steady myself against the hood of a car. The nurse closest to me put a hand out and asked, "Are you okay? Do you know where you're going?" She gestured behind her at the hospital building. The other one shaded her eyes with her hand and squinted at me, looking concerned.

"Of course I know where I'm going." I tried to lift the bag on my shoulder that contained my files, as if this was evidence of some kind, but it was a little heavy; it flopped back against my side. "I'm not a patient, I work here."

"Oh, sorry," the nurse said. To take away from the awkwardness, her friend added, "Happy solstice! Hope you have a great summer." They started walking a little faster, and I saw the first one glancing back at me as I stepped through the sliding door and into the lobby's cool air.

I sat down for a moment to savor the relief of it. The old woman who operates the convenience kiosk by the elevators was singing, as she always did. In all the years I'd been coming to the hospital, I hadn't learned her name, even though I often stopped to buy something from her– Lifesavers, a pack of gum. Her voice was frail and she didn't sing loud enough to disturb anyone in the lobby, so it's possible not everyone heard her. But I always made it a point to listen. The woman moved me, somehow. How she was still in that spot, singing and selling things, I could not fathom; she'd seemed ancient to me when I first started coming here, and that was fifteen years ago.

In the past, though I'd tried, I never managed to decipher her words or the exact tune. But now I heard clearly that she was singing "O Holy Night," despite the fact that it was morning and the first day of summer. Was she singing more loudly than usual, or was I just hearing things better than I ever had before? Had she made it a point, when she saw me, to make sure I understood?

The idea made me shiver. Usually I walk down the stairs to the Crypt, but today I took the elevator. For the first time in all the years I'd been coming to these meetings, I was glad to be going down instead of up. I didn't mind that the Crypt had no windows, because that sun was just too bright.

Of course it's not an official listing in the hospital directory, the Crypt. That's just the name we came up with for the basement conference room where we meet, a few feet down from the maintenance office. It's really just a big supply closet they took the supplies out of so they could fit in a round table and some chairs. We understand that nobody really cares about us coders—our work isn't medical in any way, and my son was right, back then, when he said it was boring. The décor doesn't matter, we're about as far from the public face of the hospital as you can get.

It was just about noon. Lily and Susannah were in the Crypt already, talking about something. When I entered, they stopped talking and looked up, both appearing surprised. "What?" I said. "It's today, right?"

"Oh, yes. Of course it is." Lily got up to pull out a chair for me. She always wears jewelry that jingles when she moves, so I heard her earrings, her necklace, and her bracelets as I sat down. "We just weren't sure you were going to make it."

"Why wouldn't I?"

They didn't look directly at each other, but I could tell they wanted to. "Roberta," Lily said. She shook her head, and there went the earrings again. She had to sweep a piece of hair from a dangling hoop. "We're so sorry."

"You didn't tell us," Susannah added, coming over to cover my shoulder with her hand. I couldn't read what was in her tone—blame, or sympathy? Probably both. I didn't like the weight of her hand on me, and I didn't like being so close to the smell of the lotion she used for her eczema, but I resisted shrugging her off.

Well, this was exactly what I had been trying to avoid—my colleagues, my *friends*, finding out before I could tell them. Last month they'd noticed that I'd lost some weight, but I explained that I'd been exercising a lot. "I was going to tell you today," I said, though this wasn't true, I'd planned to hold off as long as I could. Until it was absolutely necessary. For one reason, I needed to keep working, I need the money. For another, if I'm being honest, a part of me believed that until I had to tell them, it might not be that bad.

"Let me get you some water," Susannah said, and left the room.

"I don't need any water. Coffee's fine." But she was already gone, and it was only Lily who heard. I waved off her serving me, walked over and poured myself a mug.

On the table was the usual plate of sandwiches from the cafeteria, and she asked if I wanted one. I knew I should say yes, because I usually did, but the idea of putting anything solid in my mouth made me feel sick. I told her I'd had a big breakfast and maybe I'd be hungrier when we were done.

Dee bustled in, apologizing for being late. I told her I'd seen her in the parking lot, but she hadn't seen me. "Oh, sorry," she said, spilling her purse and notebook and files on the table a moment before they would have all dropped to the floor. "Too many balls in the air, you know?"

I did know. There was a time when this was true for me. Now, I wanted nothing more than a few balls to toss up there, even if I wouldn't be able to watch them land.

Susannah returned, setting the cup of water in front of me. We sat down and went through our agenda. I was the only one who'd screwed up this month, an audit had been triggered on one of my files. I saw where I'd made the error—well, *errors*—but it didn't seem like that big a deal to me. I was surprised they all seemed to think it was. I waited for one or more of them to say that they understood how it could happen, that they could have made the same mistake themselves, but they didn't. I decided I'd just shut up for the rest of the meeting and then leave as soon as the business part was over, if that's how they were going to be.

But when the business part was over, Susannah and Dee said they had to check on something together. When they closed the door behind them to leave me alone with

Lily, I knew what it meant.

"Roberta, I really am very sorry about this." She looked paler than usual, and when she reached to knead her temple, I saw that she'd returned to her habit of biting her fingernails when she felt stressed. "We're going to have to–*suspend*–sending you any more files, at least for the time being. It's not me, I promise, it's Corporate"–(she made her bracelets ring by pointing at the ceiling; the hospital's administration was on the top floor, ten stories above where we sat)–"they're concerned your–*faculties*–might be compromised, they're afraid they can't take that chance."

I was going to try to make a joke, about Corporate having some nerve suggesting that my faculties might be compromised, but I knew I didn't have what it took to pull it off. "That's a pretty cold way to put it," I said instead. "And what, no warning? No probation, just *pffft*, I'm fired?" I made a slicing motion across my throat.

Lily looked away from me, at a prehistoric filing cabinet whose drawers had rusted shut long ago–we know because we tried them once. Was she thinking about how nice it would feel to go outside when her shift was over, and how glad she was that she had many summer days beyond this one?

After a moment, she forced herself to meet my eyes again. "Not fired," she said quietly. "They're not firing you–you'll still be on the payroll. And if things get better, if your health–*resolves*–well, then they'll have no problem sending you files again."

But we both knew what this was all shorthand for.

We both knew what it meant.

"I really wanted to *resign*," I told her.

"You can still do that. They'll let you." She seemed eager to grant me the wish I had expressed. "Whenever you think it's time."

"Can I at least finish the files in my queue?" Thank God I'd coded Celia Santoro's before I came. I'd seen hers coming and skipped others to get to it. I would not have wanted to miss knowing what was going on with her.

"I'm sorry," Lily said again. "I was instructed to amend your access, just before you came in."

Well, I appreciated that, at least—she could have said *restricted*. Or *cut off*, or *blocked*. *Amended* was less harsh. Theoretically *amended* can move in both directions, for better or worse, whereas with *blocked* or *restricted*, there's no doubt about where you stand.

I said "Thank you," though I didn't mean it. I said, "Is that it?" meaning, if I'm not going to come to these meetings anymore, does that mean I won't see you guys again? But I couldn't bring myself to ask the real question.

She seemed to understand. "We should plan a time to get together, the four of us, outside of here." She gestured around us at the Crypt and the larger hospital grounds. "That was so fun, the dinner last year for your—" She stopped herself.

She'd been going to say "anniversary," I knew. Last summer Grettie hosted a dinner party to celebrate the one-year mark of my surgery, which we believed had cured my cancer. She invited some of the women friends we had in common, and Lily and Dee and Susannah came, too. It was nice, they all seemed genuinely happy for me, and I was touched by their toast. I even tried a variation of the old joke, which suffered a little because I'd rehearsed it in my head a few too many times, about how the surgeon had told me that beginning eight weeks after my surgery I could lift heavy items, perform strenuous exercise, and have intercourse, and how I'd said back to her, *Oh, that's good, because I wasn't having intercourse before.* All of the women laughed as if I'd delivered it like a pro, and I was touched by that, too.

It had been a good night, one of the best since my diagnosis. I could see that Lily hesitated to remind me of it now, as if maybe I'd forgotten that my situation had changed so much—become so *amended*—between then and now. "I'll call you soon," she finished, then seemed to regret that, too.

Discreetly (but I noticed), she sent off a text, and within a few seconds Dee and Susannah returned to the room. Susannah was crying. Dee's jaw was set in the way it is just before she objects to something. As cheesy as it sounds, the four of us in De Coder Ring had a group hug, and the guys in the maintenance office seemed to know what was going on, because they didn't come in and try to highjack the leftover sandwiches as they usually did. I don't remember leaving the room, though I'm sure I must have said good-bye to the guys—I'd known them all those years, too. I don't remember taking the elevator up to the lobby or hearing the old woman singing for the last time. I don't remember going out to my car or getting inside it. I only remember that the air was hotter than when I came in, and that the sun, or something, was in my eyes. I drove out of the hospital parking lot in the direction of Grettie's house, where I was counting on the bins having been emptied, so I could return them to where they belonged.

Was it only because my job had just been "amended" that I felt even more unsure of myself, driving, than I usually did? Maybe I should have taken some time at the hospital, or in the parking lot, after Lily gave me the news and before getting into my car. But I realized this too late. Instead I squinted until my eyes hurt, trying not to make a wrong move.

Sometimes I catch myself thinking that if I'd been a different kind of person—more relaxed, not such a nervous Nellie about driving and everything else—maybe I wouldn't have gotten cancer in the first place. And even if I had, the first time, maybe it wouldn't have come back now. Was it my being afraid that caused it to happen? I try not to think so, but sometimes it's hard to resist the suspicions that pop into my head.

PATIENT ID: 4559362

DIAGNOSIS: Grade II adenocarcinoma of the endo-metrium

INDICATIONS: The patient is a 45-year-old woman in otherwise good health who sought medical intervention after vaginal bleeding other than at the time of menstruation. Referred to gynecology for examination and biopsy.

HISTORY: Onset of menstruation age 12, periods have been regular to this point. Patient likely in pre-menopause. She carried one pregnancy to 36 weeks 17 years ago, premature but successful emergency C-section due to fetal distress from placental abruption.

(Is it any wonder Will suffers? He was literally in distress when he came into the world.)

OPERATION: Total laparoscopic hysterectomy, bilateral salpingo-oophorectomy, bilateral sentinel lymph node biopsy, omental biopsy, pelvic washing.

PROCEDURE: The patient was prepped and draped in the dorsal lithotomy position with pneumatic boots, antibiotics, Foley catheter, V-care and heparin. The skin was entered through an abdominal incision and a careful abdominal survey was performed. Sentinel nodes were identified and removed using the pinpoint system. The uterus, cervix, tubes, ovaries and omentum were all drawn out through the vaginal canal without difficulty.

COMPLICATIONS: There were no complications.

PATHOLOGY: Endometrial adenocarcinoma, grade 2. Slight lymphovascular space invasion is identified (multiple levels were examined on selected slides). Grade 2 is based on the presence of rare atypical, possibly serous cells but more likely of the endometrioid type.

FOLLOW-UP CARE: It is anticipated that the surgery will result in complete recovery. Possible adjuvant referral for radiation pending further examination of tumor.

I should have known right away. I'm in the medical profession, for God's sake, I'd coded enough of these stories
in the past twenty years. I saw blood in the toilet, more
than there should have been and at the wrong times. For
a day or two I tried to convince myself that it was only
a precursor to menopause, my hormones going on the
blink—what I'd heard a doctor describe once as "one last
egg in the basket." Well, then, so maybe I had multiple
last eggs. I knew it really wasn't a good sign, though, so I
called my doctor's office. When I told the nurse what was
going on, she had me come in that afternoon.

The doctor sent me straight to ob-gyn for a biopsy,
and they sped up the results out of professional courte-
sy, since I'd done their coding for years. Four days later
I got the call. "Unfortunately, they found some cancer
cells in your sample," the young gynecologist told me.
Her voice sounded fragile, and I wondered how many
times she'd had to deliver such news, either in person or
on the phone. Probably not many, in her short career. I
felt sorry for her.

Then, as with an audio delay, I heard what she had
said. After hearing it, it took me a few more seconds to
understand that "some cancer cells" = "cancer." *Some
cancer cells* was a code, I realized, intended to make the
blow a little easier when the patient registered the words.

I appreciated this. And it worked. Instead of immediate panic, I slid into understanding far more gently than
if she'd said, *You have cancer.*

I didn't tell Will at first. The diagnosis came in April
of his junior year—a little more than two years ago, now.

We'd had the worst winter in Boston of all time, almost a hundred and ten inches of snow, a bunch of blizzards and missed school days, everybody hibernating under the impression that it was never going to end. I remember that the snow in our yard came up to my chest. By the middle of March, Will was as weary of it as I was, but somehow he found what it took to keep up with and even exceed the academic goals he'd laid out for himself. Those next couple of months were important; he needed his highest grades if he had any hope of getting into the colleges he had his heart set on because of their psychobiology programs. His schoolwork had suffered from his emetophobia, though his grades were still better than those of most of his class; that's how smart he is. Still, the guidance counselor told him at the beginning of that spring semester that he'd need to buckle down and give his best effort between then and June, and I was determined to do everything I could to support him in that.

Not telling him meant, of course, that I also had to put off the surgery. But I figured a short delay like that wouldn't make a difference. The risk was worth it—I knew how disruptive it would be if I told him I was sick, he wouldn't be able to concentrate on his chemistry or his stats. I was afraid it might paralyze him.

Back when he was in middle school, around the time his stomach problems started, he told me he was afraid that if he didn't check every single thing off his long to-do list, which he refreshed every day, something bad would happen. "Like what?" I'd asked.

He shrugged, but it was a shrug filled with worry. "I don't know. Like suddenly I won't be able to do *anything*, anymore. It would be like stepping off a train track, and not being allowed to get back on."

"But honey," I said, "That's too much pressure to put on yourself. There's no train, no tracks. And even if there were, there's no such thing as not being able to get back on."

Of course, I know better now. But I didn't, back then.

"I know," he said, but I could tell it didn't help any, he still felt what he felt.

I tried again, remembering suddenly the quote on one of the tai chi posters in his bedroom. "Or I guess what I'm trying to say is, 'There's more than one path up the mountain.'"

He nodded. "Okay." I should have known he would have tried those mental strategies already, the things he'd started to learn from tai chi. He added, "Thanks," which broke my heart a little, because I knew I hadn't helped him at all.

I waited until his finals were over, then sat him down to use the same words the young gynecologist had used with me. "They found *some cancer cells*, but I'm meeting with a surgeon who'll take them out." This was the middle of June, almost exactly two years ago, now that I think about it. Two convicted murderers had broken out of a maximum-security prison in upstate New York a week earlier, and despite the intense manhunt reported all over the news, they'd managed to elude capture. One of the search members admitted in an interview that "they could be anywhere." So even though we lived a few hundred miles away, everybody was feeling a little bit tense.

When I told him that I'd had a biopsy revealing some cancer cells, Will drew his fingers into a fist. "Why'd you go to the doctor?" he asked. "Did something hurt?"

"No. I was bleeding."

"I never saw any blood. You didn't have any bandages." I recognized that this was his way of resisting what I'd told him, of suggesting that maybe the doctors were wrong.

"Well, it wasn't . . . external." I watched it dawn on him, and he flushed quickly. "Oh."

My kind of cancer was a good kind if you had to have it, I told him. Most of the time, surgery alone is a cure. The lab at the hospital had sent my sample to the surgeon I'd be seeing next week, so we'd know more then, but probably the operation would take care of it.

"I'm coming with you to the appointment," he said.

I told him he didn't have to do that, I was planning to ask Grettie.

"We'll all go." He waved away my objection like so much white noise, and I knew I couldn't deny him.

I'd told him the truth; I did plan to ask Grettie to drive me to the appointment with the surgeon. What I hadn't said was that Grettie didn't know about the cancer yet. I'd wanted to tell her, but it didn't feel right for her to know before Will did.

Who am I kidding, there was another reason, too. I waited to tell her because, same as with the night in the cemetery, I was afraid she might not have as strong a reaction to the news as I wanted—needed—her to have. I needed her to be afraid, both for and with me. I wanted to know that my cancer mattered to her not just because we were friends, but because she didn't want to lose me.

As it turned out, I got more than I was hoping for. "You've known this for *two months?*" she said, stopping cold after I managed to get the words out while we were taking the dogs for a walk. Her eyes were flashing. I know I shouldn't admit that her anger excited me, but it did.

I told her it wasn't just her, I'd waited to tell Will, too. I said I was sorry, which seemed to inflame her even more. "Don't be sorry to *me!* Be sorry to yourself, for God's sake. Be sorry to him."

I would have felt better if she'd said something like You *should* be sorry, what would I do without you? But I could tell that's what she was thinking. Or something like it.

We still hadn't resumed the walk with the dogs, who both strained against their leashes. "For God's sake, Roberta." She only ever uses my full name when she's mad at me or trying to make a point. "Since when do you keep something this big, and this scary, to yourself?"

And there it was: my Gretchen Question! I knew she had no idea about the nerve she touched—the nerve she perforated. She meant why hadn't I told her about the cancer, I got that, but to me the question went a lot deeper, and shook me to the core.

I learned about it in college, in a course on Romantic texts. The Gretchen Question—in German, *die Gretchenfrage*—is the one you don't want to answer because it exposes the thing you most want to conceal. It comes from the scene that depicts Faust refusing to answer his own Gretchen, when she asks if he believes in God. He hems and haws his response, because he can't let her know he's made a deal with the Devil.

The original Gretchenfrage was about religion, but my professor said it became more general over time. So for one person, the Gretchen Question might be "You're telling me you chose wine over having children?" For another, "Did you recognize the harm you were causing, but went ahead anyway?"

The stakes in a Gretchen Question are high, when you go to answer. Telling the truth is risky; you might give too much of yourself away.

And what was my answer? Not to her question about the cancer—that one was easy, I just said it had been a shock, I needed time to absorb it for myself.

But I couldn't stop thinking about the other thing, the thing Grettie didn't know enough to ask about. The truth I'd never told anyone. What I really wanted to say to her was *If you only knew!*

I met her as a freshman at UMass, answering the ad she placed for a roommate in the apartment she rented when she began her graduate program in political science. I was too late for a dorm assignment because we hadn't thought I could afford to go to college, but at the last minute my mother asked her aunt for more money and then there I was, needing a place to live.

I saw immediately that Grettie was a different creature from me. It wasn't just that she was so smart, although that was part of it. She'd grown up in New York

City, eating in Thai and Indian and Vietnamese restaurants. Central Massachusetts, where I grew up, was not all that far away in terms of miles, but the closest I'd come to an international meal was stir-fry in a Styrofoam container from the Chinese counter in the food court at our mall. Grettie had traveled to Europe and Asia. She was not afraid to try things like snorkeling, and she had double-pierced ears.

Part of it had to do with money, of course. But it was more than that: the real difference had to do with how she carried herself, and how she moved through the world. I tended to hunch over, sit toward the back of rooms, and do my best to shrink. The therapist told me once that when he looked at me, he saw a person who didn't believe she deserved the space she occupied. What could I tell him? He was right.

But Grettie: she walked tall with her shoulders back, took in whatever she needed, and plopped her body and belongings down in the middle of whatever room she entered. She was a center in herself. How better to say it? I wanted to orbit her.

My luck in finding the ad, then being chosen by her, was something I felt grateful for every day. (I still do.) Over pizza in our kitchen the night I learned about Faust's Gretchen, I asked if that's where her name had come from. No, Grettie said, though she knew the story, despite the fact that her field was politics and not literature. She told me her parents had named her for the Clever Gretchen in an old European fairy tale. "And thank God," she added, "the Faust one kills her baby and goes insane, right?" I nodded, knowing she must be right—she knew so much, she was so clever—though we hadn't reached that part of the story in class.

Even in college, even without knowing what the question would be, I hoped that someone would care enough about me to ask me *die Gretchenfrage* someday. That it turned out to be Grettie seemed perfectly right and made me feel all the more grateful, even though I couldn't show it in any way. *Since when do you keep something this big, and this scary, to yourself?* I had to do the same as Faust, avoid giving an answer. Hem and haw. Of course Grettie noticed, but by then the dogs were pulling us, and the question got lost in the bustle along the path.

She and Will and I went into the city together to meet with the surgeon my medical friends had told me was the best. The room they showed us to, to wait for her, was so tiny it only had an examining table and one chair. I sat on the table, Grettie sat on the chair, and Will leaned against the wall next to the hazardous-materials bin. When the surgeon and her intern entered, Grettie gave up her seat, and I could see how agitated she felt that there was no room for her to pace even a few steps as we all waited for Dr. Venn to speak.

They'd had their pathologists review the biopsy, she told me—standard procedure when they received a sample from somewhere else. A team of six pathologists altogether, she said, had taken a second look.

"Six," Grettie exhaled, and I knew it had been involuntary; she would have kept it in if she could. Against the wall, Will made a little movement with his arms—the beginning of one of his tai chi postures, I saw—then quickly folded them as if otherwise they'd continue with a mind of their own.

Embrace the Moon, I knew that motion was called. Every time I saw Will do it, I thought of a pregnant woman cradling her belly. The pull-cord for emergencies dangled right next to his arm, and when I had a sudden vision of him giving it a violent yank, I gasped a little myself.

"That's not unusual," Dr. Venn said, misreading the reason for my gasp. They liked to make sure there was agreement, she added. The six pathologists had almost come to terms—only one wouldn't sign off—in concluding that the cells in my sample were the most benign kind, well-differentiated and less likely to metastasize than the two other types. She pulled out a little chart and pointed to the different cell images. Instead of really focusing on them I asked, "Ha, is that your Venn diagram?" and she tried her best to give me a little smile. Behind her, I saw Grettie biting her lip.

She would do the surgery the following week or the week after, Dr. Venn told me; she'd have her scheduler call. And we'd know more after that, because at that point they'd have the whole tumor to look at.

Did we have any questions? The surgeon turned to include Grettie and Will.

Will asked, "Is she going to die?" Too late to do any good, I shook my head at him.

"He's just worried," I told the surgeon. "He knows you can't answer that."

Will said, "No, I don't."

Dr. Venn smiled at all of us, but I could tell she hadn't expected this direct question from my son. "We don't have an overwhelming reason to think that's something we have to consider right now. It depends on what the lab says about the type of cells we find, but we're hoping your mom won't need anything further after the surgery. Possibly a mild course of radiation, but it may be that all she needs are follow-up exams for five years. You're in high school, right? What year?"

"Senior. In the fall," Will said.

"Well, then, let's hope that by the time you graduate from college, her follow-ups will be just about over, and she can go back to seeing her primary once a year. This will all be a distant memory."

How I wish, now, that she hadn't said that! She'd been cautious: *We don't have an overwhelming reason. It may be. Let's hope.* But of course it was everything that followed those words that Will focused on. *Your mom won't need anything further.* I could tell that he and Grettie were relieved, and I allowed myself to feel it, too. "In the meantime, let's take things a step at a time," Dr. Venn said. "Okay?"

She was asking all of us to let her and the intern go. Grettie and I thanked her; Will stared at her but said nothing, which seemed to unnerve the surgeon a little. When we were alone in the room again, Grettie said, "I think it all sounds pretty encouraging. And she's scheduling the surgery soon, which is good."

"Yes." None of us wondered out loud if scheduling it

soon might mean something to worry about. "I can't wait to get it over with."

Grettie and Will took care of me together. The surgery was on June twenty-eighth, the same day the police arrested the second of the escaped convicts in New York; they'd shot and killed the first guy two days earlier, not even fifty miles from the prison. Only fifty miles, after being on the lam for three weeks! I took this as a good omen, a kind of metaphor: the cancer cells had broken out in my body and caused some trouble, there was a panic, but they didn't get very far before they were captured, everybody would be safe now.

Grettie picked us up early in the morning to make the treacherous rush-hour drive into Boston, which she never seems to mind. She's driven in Rome and Australia, and she scoots around in her brother-in-law's Citroën whenever they go over to Ireland—it's nothing to her, whereas I just wait for every car coming in the opposite direction to swerve into mine. Like I said, nervous Nellie.

The hospital my surgery was performed in is nothing like the small one I do—did—the coding for, it's like an entire city within itself. Will and Grettie waited nearly all day for me while I was in pre-op, surgery, and the recovery room. Later, I asked him how they'd spent all those hours. Playing games in the family lounge, he told me: checkers, Monopoly, Crazy Eights. What did you talk about? I asked.

He shrugged. "You know. You, the surgery. How long would it take, how long before the anesthesia would wear off, stuff like that. Just, whatever."

Grettie had a different story, though I could tell she hesitated to mention it, with me in my fragile state. But I told her I could handle it, I wanted to know. She sighed and said, "Okay. He asked if I could tell him anything about his father." When I gave a start, she said, "See? I should have waited to tell you."

"No, it's fine. I'm just surprised, that's all." I said that he hadn't asked me anything about his father in years. I thought he'd forgotten about it, or given it up. "What did you say?"

She held her palms up in front of her, as if to show that her hands had been empty, she'd had nothing to offer my son. "What *could* I? I told him I didn't know anything more than he did—that you used a sperm bank, that it was all anonymous, and that there was no way to track him down."

I slumped back in my seat. Of course she couldn't have told him anything other than these things, but I still felt relief. "I don't know why he insists on using the word 'father,'" I said. "*Jack's* a father. What Will had was a donor. But you try telling him that."

I could see that she had more to say, but wasn't sure she should. "Go ahead," I told her.

"It's just that I don't understand why *you* don't understand. 'Father' is the correct word, the biological word. The social word. Whatever you want to call it. The guy fathered him." She paused, and I watched her mind continue to move behind those eyes I loved. "I don't understand why you keep saying there's nothing you can tell him. You get that he's not asking for a name, right? Or an address or anything. He's asking for whatever code they assigned the donor, however the sperm bank kept track."

I looked away and told her, "I don't have it anymore."

Now she was the one who seemed shocked. "Well," she said, and I could tell she was saving the question of *Why* for another time, "you may not have it, but they would. He'd settle for knowing what clinic you went to. Give him that, and you're off the hook—they'll be the ones to tell him he's out of luck, if he inquires, because the donor didn't agree to be contacted. Right?"

I made my murmuring noise, the one that could have meant Yes or No or anything in between. Grettie knows that noise. Sometimes she calls me on it, sometimes she doesn't. This time she didn't, probably because I was recovering. But I knew it didn't mean she wouldn't ask me again sometime on Will's behalf, which she had no reason to think was not on my own behalf, too.

Was this why I'd never told her about it, both when I got pregnant and ever since? Because I anticipated that precisely this situation might arise someday—she'd be sitting around just chatting with Will, and he'd ask her what she knew about his father, and by not telling her anything I was saving her, in that potential moment, from having to make the same choice I'm facing now?

Not to mention the threat to him if she *did* know, made the wrong choice, and told him.

Since when do you keep something this big, and this scary, to yourself? I've been tempted to tell her, so many times. The truth is that I was just too afraid. Ashamed. Afraid. Well, both. Ashamed of what she would think of me. Afraid she'd want me to do something, when back then I didn't have what it took.

Now, it feels too late to say anything. I need her too much. I can't take the chance that it would change things between us, her knowing I've lied for so long.

And I should have realized that I'd been stupid, naïve, not to understand how important it would be to Will. After my surgery, when Grettie told me he still wanted to know, I should have cut it off at the pass—his wish. I should have brought up the subject we hadn't mentioned between us for years, and reminded him that there was no revelation forthcoming, because there couldn't be.

But I didn't do it. First because I was weak from surgery, then because every time I imagined having the conversation with him, I was afraid of what it would do to him. I was afraid the emetophobia would come back.

Who am I kidding, I was also afraid he'd hate me. And I was right to think it, because look at where we are now.

I wasn't forced to drive the alternate route to Grettie's house—there was no sign of whatever problem had shut down the highway on my way up to the hospital, and all lanes were open now—but I didn't trust myself on the fast road, given how shaky I felt over being shut out of my queue. Well, let's face it, about losing my job. Not that it came as all that big a surprise, but thinking something might happen and actually *having* it happen are always two different things.

So I retraced my trip along the back roads, which was slightly longer but much prettier than the highway. I should have taken this route to and from the hospital the whole time, I thought, feeling moved by all the green around me as I drove past school fields and neighborhoods lined with old trees, an old-fashioned garden stand (*Fay's Fresh Flowers!*) and even a couple of horse pastures. Now, it's too late.

I like summers more now than I did when I was depressed—on sunny days back then, all I could think about were happy people doing happy things, and how far I was from them—but fall has always been my favorite. And I can't help feeling cheated, because last fall was so awful, and here I am probably not going to get another chance.

Technically the trouble started during the summer, just before Will left for college. It still pulls me up short to realize I've only seen him once since then, when he brought home his girlfriend Sosi for the long weekend of his Thanksgiving break.

"What kind of a name is Sosi?" I said, when he called to tell me (tell, not ask) that she was coming. I hadn't even known he had a girlfriend.

He took offense, assuming, I could tell, that I was re-acting to the foreignness of it. It's true that it sounded kind of New Age-y to me, and I'm not the biggest New Age fan. But what I really meant was, Where does the name come from? I was genuinely interested. When I clarified, he said, "Her family's Armenian. It means some kind of tree."

I didn't want a stranger in the house for four days, but, more, I didn't want to alienate him further, so I said I was looking forward to meeting her. "We're going to stay in my room," he replied, in a voice that was the tonal equivalent of a chin raised in defiance.

Fine, I said, though I didn't mean that I was fine with it—what I meant was that I would not object. I told him I would let Grettie know that we were bringing an extra person to Thanksgiving dinner. "Oh, that reminds me, she's vegan," Will said. He told me, further, that Sosi was allergic to dogs. Could I arrange to put Scout in the kennel that weekend? Fine, I said again, although this also took me aback.

After we hung up, I went to the computer to find out exactly what a vegan was, and what one could eat. Then I went into Will's bedroom. We've lived here since he was a baby, when Grettie pulled some strings and got my name approved for the list of first tenants in this small townhouse complex that combines rentals with condo units—it's pretty much the only place you can live in this town without having to own. I was thrilled at the idea of bringing Will up here, because the schools are so good. (Well, who am I kidding, also because Grettie was nearby.) There'd been three beds in Will's room since then: crib, big-boy bed, and then the full-size double we brought in when he was in middle school, after we painted the room together. A dark green. It would have been too dark for me, but he said the color made him feel like he was sleeping in a forest. "Is that a good thing?" I asked, and he looked at me as if he thought I might be joking. "Of course it is," he said.

He had taken down all the old posters (Shrek, Buzz Lightyear) and after we repainted he put up two new ones, both reflecting the spirit of tai chi. *Yield and overcome* was one of the captions; the other was the quote about there being more than one path up the mountain. He'd started taking tai chi classes the year before at the suggestion of his pediatrician, who thought it might help with his asthma. Practicing the full and deep breaths of tai chi can stimulate the lungs, the doctor told us, and increase the amount of air flowing in and out, eventually reducing asthma's overall effects. It sounded like a stretch to me (I'm afraid I might even have used the term *New Age* in a scornful way), but I found a beginner's class for Will at the community center, and to my surprise, he took to it right away.

Tai chi turned out to be perfect for him, because he'd never liked ball sports, he didn't have the best eye-hand coordination, he didn't get picked for teams in gym class until the very end. With tai chi, he didn't have to worry about letting anyone down. And he could do it whenever he wanted—he didn't need a field or a court or any equipment, just his body and a knowledge of the right moves.

I was glad he'd found a sport he liked, although he had to correct me at first; it wasn't a "sport"—it was a *practice*. It was a mental discipline, as much as it was physical.

Yes, it's exercise, he said, but you're not supposed to work hard. It's supposed to be easy. You're supposed to go as slow as you possibly can, and when you think you can't go any slower, you slow down some more. He said, Isn't that a relief?

I know why he said that, about *easy* being a relief. From the time he was little I told him about something my own mother had taught my sister and me, beginning right after our father left: if every morning you could do something difficult, it would give you a feeling of accomplishment and put you in a confident mood for the rest of the day. My mother's method was to take a shower before breakfast, with water as cold as she could bear. My sister called bullshit on that—not literally, we weren't allowed to swear, but she thought it sounded nuts. Even though my mother sometimes poured her first drink right after that shower (not that we were supposed to notice; it was supposed to look like regular orange juice), I believed for most of my life what our mother told us. It made sense to me. It was why I always took eight a.m. classes in college, and why, until I got sick, I liked to exercise first thing and get it out of the way.

The class Will took was called Meditation in Motion. I was intrigued, I admit, and I loved the names he taught me of the different postures: *Repulse the Monkey, Rooster Stands on One Leg, Snake Creeps Through the Grass.* They sound like little stories in themselves. I guess that's how they originated, in China, all those centuries ago.

One day Will asked me to do a two-person posture with him called *Push Hands.* The object is to upset your opponent's balance while maintaining your own. He showed me a video first, to give me an idea of what it should look like. "But it's not fair," I said, "I'm so much bigger than you are. I don't want to make you fall."

In fact I wasn't actually that much bigger, by then. He's on the short side but so am I, and it had taken me longer than it should have to realize he'd almost caught up to me. A sly smile came over his face when I said what I did, and he told me, "You won't." We stood across from each other in the living room and tried it. "You want to sink down as low as you can," he told me. "It helps keep you rooted and signals humility. Also, the higher a person stands, the easier she is to knock over."

Why did he say "she," I wondered? I was the one who kept losing my balance, and it made me annoyed. "It will work better if you stop trying so hard," Will said, and that annoyed me, too.

I couldn't understand why he'd asked me to do this particular exercise with him. Did he want to show that he could knock me off center, get the upper hand on me— literally—every time?

It flustered me. I felt foolish. Afterward he said, "You might want to try a class yourself sometime, Mom. A lot of older people take it up because it helps with balance and proprioception. That means knowing where you are in the space around you, even when you have your eyes closed. It helps you stay stable."

"I know what proprioception means," I said, though the truth was that I would not have been able to articulate a definition.

"It's also really good for your core."

Maybe someday I'd look into it, I told him. When I was an "older person." I hoped he might smile at that, but he didn't. Instead he shook his head a little, but I saw that it was with affection. Soon afterward he took to practicing in his room instead of in the living room, where he'd started out when he didn't mind me watching.

Preparing for their visit I pictured him and his girl-friend in the bed together, even though I had never seen a photo and didn't know what she looked like. Will's window gives out onto the courtyard we share with the other units in the quad. When he was younger we used to spend a lot of time in the yard, having picnics or sitting on the small bench to read together, but we stopped do-ing those things when he started middle school; now that I think about it, that year was a real turning point for us, the ending of some things and the beginning of others. Before then, when the subject of his father came up, it always included the question of whether Will could find out who that man was. If he could meet him. When he first asked, I told him that I was sorry but it was impossible, because I had used an anonymous donor. I explained what that meant. Even *I* didn't know who it was, I said.

But that didn't stop him from making up stories, or from searching the world. "Look at that man," he'd say, if we were out somewhere and he saw a small boy reaching up to hold his father's hand on the way into a store or a restaurant. "Maybe that's him." When I said No, I didn't think so, Will said, "But you said you don't know who it is, right? So it could be him. It could."

I had no choice but to say Yes, it was possible, but very unlikely. It pleased him to hear me say this, I saw. It happened more times than I could keep track of. Shortly after he began taking the tai chi lessons, he stopped asking, and stopped pointing out fathers and sons. I dared to feel relieved; I thought he'd replaced his first obsession with another, healthier one, or come around to understanding that we all have questions we'll never get answered. Until Grettie told me after my surgery that he was still waiting for a revelation, and a year later he brought it up himself on his eighteenth birthday, triggering the rupture we still haven't recovered from.

There's a big elm tree in the middle of the yard, its branches hanging over the bench. I imagined Sosi looking out from the bed and saying it looked like a giant umbrella.

But no, I remembered—it was I who used to say that. And it only looked like an umbrella when it had its leaves, which were gone now at the end of November.

They were scheduled to arrive on Wednesday night in plenty of time for dinner, so I looked up some vegan recipes online and settled on a fettuccini Alfredo, with mushroom sauce instead of meat. I was happy to find it because fettuccini Alfredo is Will's favorite, and this way I would be taking both of their wishes into account. He would appreciate that, wouldn't he? Wouldn't they both? I had it in the oven baking at five o'clock; he'd told me to expect them around six.

But at six-forty-five, after I'd put the meal on warm and had to tide myself over with cheese and crackers, he called to say they were going to be delayed. The traffic is terrible, he said.

That's okay, what time, then? I asked. He said he felt bad about this, but they probably weren't going to make it there until after I went to bed.

It didn't make sense, because their school was less than three hours away in regular traffic, and he'd told me they planned to start the drive after lunch. I wouldn't be going to bed for another four hours. But I didn't say any of this—I just told him I'd made them dinner, and they could eat whenever they got here. Just stick it in the microwave, I said. He thanked me, but when I got up on Thanksgiving morning, I saw that it hadn't been touched.

Nevertheless, I was determined to present myself as a mother my son could be proud of. The girl came out of the bedroom first, yawning, wearing a pair of his flannel pajama bottoms and a flesh-colored camisole. Her hair—she was a redhead, which surprised me, I would have thought he'd have mentioned this—was a wild tumble around her face, so that at first I could barely make out her features. I introduced myself and said I hoped she'd slept well. I told her I hadn't heard them come in last night; they must have been very quiet. In saying this I was trying to reassure her that if they had done anything intimate in his room, I hadn't been aware of it. But I'm not sure she picked up on my intention. "He didn't want you to wake up," she said, putting out a thin hand to shake mine. "I'm really glad to meet you. I've heard so many things."

What kind of things I could only imagine, but I tried to put them out of my mind.

"He looks like you. And you're so pretty!" she exclaimed, as if she were only now just noticing, or just now realizing that this would be a nice thing to say. "He didn't tell me that."

I mumbled a thank you and said it probably wasn't the type of things boys said about their mothers. When she turned to head to the bathroom, I looked at my reflection in the microwave and couldn't help a little smile.

I was glad she hadn't called me Roberta or, worse, Bert. She didn't call me Mrs. Chase, either. She didn't call me anything, which I guess was for the best.

I turned on the TV, hoping that the Macy's parade might have started, but it was too early. When he was little this had been Will's favorite part of Thanksgiving; he enjoyed the parade even more than going to Grettie and Jack's house to play in the woods with Cam.

He came out of the bedroom before Sosi finished her shower. I was making scrambled eggs, and he looked into the pan and said, "You know she can't eat those, right?"

"Oh, damn," I said. I'd forgotten about the egg part

of vegan. "Well, there's toast, too. *You'll* eat the eggs with me, though, right?"

He answered that he didn't know, he thought he'd rather not, maybe he'd just have coffee and save his appetite for dinner. "But I've put six eggs in here," I said.

He shrugged. "You can save the rest."

We heard the shower stop, and I pushed the pan to a cold burner. I stepped closer to him to make sure Sosi wouldn't hear us, and did my best to ignore seeing that as I did so, he took a step away. "Are we going to have any time just the two of us?" I whispered. "This weekend?"

"Why, do you have something to say to me?" He looked amused, as if he already knew my answer and it was the lame one he expected me to give. His expression sliced through my heart. "Did you change your mind?"

I hesitated about how to respond to this. I did have something to tell him—something that would change everything—but it was not what he wanted to hear.

The bathroom door opened and Sosi emerged, toweling her tumble of hair. "Anything you have to say to me, you can say in front of Sosi," Will said. "It's really only because of her that we came here this weekend. You have her to thank for that."

I mumbled something that could have been taken as *Thank you.*

Sosi looked from him to me. "You don't have to thank me. I just hated that you guys weren't speaking. But I don't want to get in the way of anything private."

"It's okay." Will set a plate of toast down in front of her. "I'm sure she's just planning to give her canned speech about anonymous donors—again. And guess what, I don't need to hear that. Again."

Well, this was not a good start to the morning, I guess it goes without saying. But I kept trying. "So, Sosi. You're Armenian!" I didn't intend to sound so excited about it. Partly I was trying to hide the fact that I knew nothing about Armenia, aside from the fact that there had been a genocide there. Now it was clear to all of us, if it hadn't been before, how hard I had to work to welcome this new person to the house I was accustomed to sharing only with my son.

"Well, my family is. My name is." She spread a prim pat of peanut butter (after checking the label) on her toast. "But I'm pretty sure I don't have a drop of it, myself."

I looked from one to the other of them, thinking for a split second that they were playing a joke on me. The pain of it, that possibility, exploded inside my chest. Then Will said, "She's adopted."

Sosi nodded confirmation as she lifted her toast and let my son take a bite from it. I looked away, as if they'd just performed a French kiss in front of me. "At first I was only a foster. Then I guess I grew on them." She smiled the smile of someone accustomed to being chosen, then pointed pertly at Will. "He thinks I should get one of those DNA kits and find out what I am. Maybe even find my birth parents. But I'm not really interested. What difference would it make?"

I tried to keep my voice under control as I asked, "You can find your birth parents with those kits?" The question was just to buy some time, because I already knew the answer. I'd looked into it, wanting to be ready for when—not if—the subject came up. But expecting something to happen is not the same as having it happen, and I felt blindsided.

He'd found the same information I had. "It's possible. Not likely, but there *are* people who've found the fathers they were looking for." He paused to let sink in for me—as if I didn't know it already!—how much he wished he were one of them. "In case you're wondering, I'm thinking of getting one of those kits myself."

"Oh, I don't think that's a good idea." I got up from the table to clatter my plate into the sink. "Why spend the money, and get your hopes up, if it's such a long shot?"

"Because a long shot is still a shot," he said. "Which is more than I get by asking you." His tone wasn't mean, even though the words were. He had a little crumb at the edge of his lip and I was going to let him know, but Sosi did it before I could and he used his napkin to blot it away.

"We've been through this," I murmured, as if using a softer tone would make the conversation less tense. "Do we have to bring it up now? You used to agree with me that it didn't matter."

"That was when I was a stupid kid. Of course I had to agree with you. What choice did I have?" He was looking straight at me as he asked this, holding up his knife as if he might use it to catch any response I tossed in his direction.

But I didn't give him one. I'd responded so many times already, and he'd never liked what he heard, so why put us both through that again? After a few minutes Sosi said, "Well, I'm not doing it. I like having a blank slate. That way there's nothing to live up to, or to live down. I'd rather just create myself, thank you." There may have been a touch of defiance in her voice along with the pride, but I didn't know her well enough yet to be sure.

"What about how you're raised?" I focused on my juice glass as I spoke, counting the pieces of pulp at the bottom. "What about *nurture*? I thought that was a lot more important. Honey, it is."

"Mom, calm down." I think he may have thought he was hurting my feelings, implying that my nurturing wasn't good enough or something. "It's just—well, not everything can be overcome or undone by your environment. You can't change your DNA."

I knew that no good could come of prolonging this conversation. When I began too quickly to clear the dishes, I knocked my glass from the table, and Will put his hand out to catch it, just in time. "Whoa, that was a phew," I said, speaking with too much cheer again, this time out of relief. If the glass had fallen and shattered, I don't know what I would have done.

"A few what?" asked Sosi, so I explained how it came from when he was a little boy and we used to play Chutes and Ladders. The whole game, Will was anxious about what would happen when he got to the last row and feared spinning the number that would force him to slide his game-piece all the way back to the beginning. "That

was a phew," he'd say when he avoided that number, hopping his piece over the fatal entrance to the chute. It became an inside phrase between us, whenever one or both of us had a reason to feel relieved.

"She doesn't know about that?" I asked him after he saved the glass from smashing, when Sosi asked A few what?

"No," he said. "I haven't told her every single silly little thing about my life."

That hurt, the word "silly," I admit. But I didn't say so. Instead I did the dishes and turned on the parade, but Will said it was too childish and changed the channel to CNN. We weren't due at Grettie and Jack's until noon, but at eleven I found myself in my bedroom calling her to whisper that we might be there a little early, if that was okay. "What's she like?" Grettie asked. "I'm dying to meet her."

"She has a lot of red hair," I said, knowing that if I added anything else it would come across as snarky, and I didn't want Grettie to think of me that way. When we got to their house everyone greeted Sosi warmly, and in hugging her Grettie said, "Any girlfriend of my godson is a goddaughter of mine." How long had she had that line prepared, I wondered? And why did it make me feel guilty?

Because I did not feel that Sosi was in any way my daughter, I suppose. I reminded myself that it was just a nice thing Grettie had thought to say—as she always did.

Though her son Cam was the only one of the kids of legal drinking age, Grettie offered a glass of beer or wine to all of them except Bella, who'd just turned twelve and who got only a cordial-sized serving of Cabernet.

I never liked Thanksgiving until I met Grettie. After my father left it was always just my mother and sister and me, with my mother trying to re-create the table decorations she saw in the photographs of *Woman's Day* and *Ladies Home Journal.* She always started drinking too early in the process, so nothing ever worked out, and we ended up eating soup and Saltines on tray tables in front of our ancient Sylvania console.

But now I hadn't missed a Thanksgiving with Grettie in more than twenty-five years. When the kids were young, Jack took them out to play in the woods or, when they were older, to run in the local Turkey Trot, while Grettie and I stayed behind at their house and talked our way through the time it took us to prepare the meal. I got my fill of her then; it was a long weekend from her college teaching so she was not in a hurry, she was not distracted, she was not on her way to someplace else.

I can think of no other time that I have ever felt as comforted or as comfortable as in Grettie's kitchen on Thanksgiving Day. I looked forward to it for weeks ahead of time, and felt the loss of it, and her, for weeks after.

But today, when Grettie was pouring people's drinks, it became obvious that there wasn't a plan for Jack to take the "kids" anywhere. Realizing that I would not have the chance to be alone with Grettie caused my stomach to constrict in resentment at Sosi. I knew it wasn't directly her fault. But I didn't care—that was what I felt.

Sosi took the Cabernet, too. Cam and Will chose

beer. All of us stayed in the kitchen and talked about the election we'd just been so shocked by—what else? At least, I was relieved to see, Sosi felt the same way about Trump as the rest of us, though I noticed she said less about him than we did. When we'd exhausted all of our outrage, we shifted gears and talked about what the kids were doing at school. Cam obviously found Sosi appealing—she flirted with him a little, tossing that wild red hair as she laughed—and I saw that this made Will feel proud instead of flustered. He was sure of her, I saw.

From the way Jack made it a point to keep his physical distance and to use more formal language than usual when he spoke to her, I knew he was trying to conceal his own attraction to his vibrant young guest. Bella, accustomed even at her tender age to being the quiet beauty in any room, had the air about her, after a few minutes, of conceding this particular room to the louder, more animated beauty among us.

Even Grettie's hostess expression of attentive interest was more attentive and interested than I'd seen in a long time. This, I admit, did make me jealous.

It was the whole family's reaction to Sosi that told me what a catch Will had made in her, and that this went far beyond her looks.

By the time we sat down in the dining room, having shared the job of carrying things out to the table, we were all a little buzzed. Before we'd even passed all the dishes around, Sosi had gotten up from the table to go into the kitchen and refill her wineglass. Grettie caught my eye and smiled, and I figured she was remembering all those nights in our Amherst apartment, when we shared those cheap bottles of Gallo and sprawled next to each other on the sofa to watch *Cagney & Lacey* or *Falcon Crest*.

There was a little bit of awkwardness around the grace. A long time ago, Jack had taught us all a Gaelic blessing, in Gaelic, that we'd taken to reciting together even though the rest of us didn't really understand what the words meant, it was more a phonetic memory exercise than anything else. In years past Will said it along with everyone at the table, but this time I noticed that he and Sosi smiled at each other and even traded winks at the sound of the lilting syllables that were pretty much gibberish to all of us except Jack. It made me feel bad; were they mocking him and his heritage? His faith? Our tradition? I decided not to think so—it was just an exchange of intimacy they thought no one else would see.

The conversation that had flowed so easily, in the kitchen, seemed to have died on the way to the dining room. Probably it was the pressure of sitting in high-backed chairs at fancy place settings, and an awareness that we were now officially Celebrating the Holiday. (It was not lost on me that Grettie's Thanksgiving table was always the one my mother aspired to, right down to the homemade pinecone-and-cranberry centerpiece.) Gamely, Grettie asked Sosi where she was from. Why hadn't I thought to ask her that myself? Because I was too busy watching her, I realized. Watching and measuring the effect she had on my son.

West Virginia, as it turned out. "Really?" Cam's interest, already high, appeared to spike. "What do your ..." He'd been about to ask what her parents did, we all understood, but then reconsidered when it occurred to him that the question might be a little too pointed.

But it didn't seem to bother Sosi. "Court clerk and meter reader," she said, and though it wasn't clear which parent did what, she offered no elaboration and nobody followed up. Were they having Thanksgiving at home today, or going somewhere else? Cam asked, and this seemed to light a fire under her, because she launched into a narrative of what was no doubt going on at that very moment in her family's dining room down in Pleasants County. Her father would have prepared a beer-can turkey on the grill, she told us. The table would be crowded with cousins and uncles and aunts. After the blessing and before the dishes were passed, her mother would whisper "FHB," short for "Family Hold Back," so that Sosi's father and brothers would wait to make sure the guests all had full plates, before serving themselves. When Bella asked why, Sosi just shrugged and said it was an expression from the old days, used when there's not a whole lot of money for extra food.

At our Thanksgiving table, nobody seemed to know what to say to this. But Sosi herself came to our rescue. "It's kind of ridiculous, because everybody sitting there knows exactly what 'FHB' means. It's not like it's some secret code. But everyone pretends she didn't say anything, or that they didn't hear." And her father and brothers, she added, would obey her mother and hold back.

"So did your family vote for Trump, then?" Bella

asked, and I could feel most of the stomachs in the room drop to exactly the same sharp point. Will laughed, though I assumed it was out of nervousness.

"Bella," Grettie said. "We don't ask things like that."

"Why not?" She seemed genuinely puzzled.

"Actually, I think they probably did." Sosi took a substantial gulp of her wine. "My parents hate Hillary."

I must have made a noise I hadn't intended, because everyone looked at me. "It doesn't matter how her parents voted," Will said, in a louder than usual voice. "She's her own person. They don't tell her what to do."

"Of course not," Grettie said, nodding with too much vigor. "Sosi, since you're majoring in sociology, are you interested in voting trends by demographic? One of my students did a great presentation on that, I could send you the link if you want."

Before Sosi could respond, Cam said, "Or maybe your specialty is globalization? Or environmental health?" He didn't seem to care that we all recognized his showing off what he knew about the field she'd chosen. "I'm guessing you aren't into the criminal side of things."

Sosi smiled. "What makes you say that? The criminal mind is really fascinating, don't you think? I'm going to do my thesis on murderers. Stranglers, specifically. How much they enjoy that moment when they see the life go out of their victim's eyes."

Everyone stopped eating. Even Will looked as if he didn't know how to react.

"I'm kidding!" Sosi laughed and reached for her

wineglass. "You guys. You should have seen your faces, that was hilarious. No, my real interest is in families. Specifically, the way they communicate. Or, more specifically, the way they don't."

Grettie asked, "Really? How so?"

"Oh boy," Will said. "We should probably go back to the subject of Donald Trump." He was trying to sound playful, but I could tell that his warning was real, and I felt gravy clot in my throat.

"I wouldn't mind hearing more," Cam said. "What about the way families communicate, or don't?"

Too late, Sosi seemed to register Will's caution. "Oh, I don't know," she said, giving an equivocal wave. "It's different for every family. I don't want to ruin Thanksgiving dinner. Forget I said anything."

"No fair." Cam shook his head, too vigorously. "Come on—you're the one who brought it up."

When no one else weighed in with an objection, Sosi put her fork down and took a breath. When she exhaled, I smelled wine. "Well, it's not really anything everybody doesn't already know. Just that most families seem inclined to avoid certain topics, to preserve the peace. Or the *illusion* of peace."

I got up and went into the kitchen to pour an inch more of wine into my own glass—just an inch—but I could still hear her. "I mean, it makes sense, I get it, but I think we'd all be better off if we were willing to talk about the hard things."

Bella asked, "Like what?"

This *will* ruin dinner, I thought.

Sosi sighed, giving the impression of a person being forced to give testimony against her will. But it was a
false impression, I was sure. I had the feeling she secretly loved this. "Well, for instance, aren't there questions
you'd ask your parents, if you thought they'd be willing
to answer them? And if you really wanted to hear what
those answers would be?"

In the expression on Bella's face then, we all watched
the train of thought traveling through her mind, before
it stopped at some station she hadn't realized lay ahead.

Enough, I said to Sosi with my own mind, but of
course she didn't hear me. To Bella she continued, "You
know, like, *Did it ever cross your mind to wish you didn't
have children?*" She swept her hand between Bella and
her brother. "*Which one of us is your favorite? Or* if you
want to go full *Sophie's Choice, which one of us would
you save, if you could only save one?*"

At the head of the table, Jack appeared a bit stunned.
He cleared his throat and said, "I think there's a perfectly good reason people don't ask each other those questions. What would be the point?"

Will said, "The truth," seeming to have forgotten his
reluctance for the subject.

Jack was usually pretty temperate, but I could tell he
was annoyed by the anxiety his daughter had been forced
to feel at the holiday table. He turned to Sosi and asked,
"You're telling me this is an actual field of research? The
things people in families don't torture each other with?"

She smiled as if he'd made a good-natured joke, before recognizing the irritation that lay behind it. "Well,

that's not how I would put it, but yes." I suppose she could be admired for standing her ground after such a question. "I wanted to find something for my thesis that no one else would be doing."

Jack laughed, not in a nice way. "Do you think there might be a reason for that?"

Across from him, Grettie warned him with her eyes to back off. Gamely Sosi answered, "I don't know, I just think our families are the ones who're supposed to have our backs. If we can't trust *them*, then who can we?" But for the first time all day, she sounded unsure of herself. I tried to ignore the look she shot at Will and the one he responded with.

I could just picture the two of them having their first conversation at school, sometime after that awful day I dropped him off. Was it in a class? Over a vegan meal in the cafeteria? They hadn't said how they met, exactly.

But I had a clear vision of her telling him she was interested in the secrets people in families kept from each other, and Will's ears perking up because what she was saying struck his most basic chord. Or maybe it happened the other way around—maybe he told her about the conflict between him and me, and it gave her the idea for her thesis. However it happened, I was pretty sure that his resentment toward me had, if not created, then sealed the bond between them. So it was my own fault this cheeky redhead had invaded our Thanksgiving.

A heavy silence fell over the table, and Sosi must have realized she was responsible, because she apologized. Will and Grettie and Cam rushed to assure her that she had nothing to feel sorry for. Then Will said, "How 'bout those Mets?" and I laughed, longer than I should have.

We fumbled our way back to benign territory. Jack, God love him, asked Will what his plans were for the summer, once classes ended. "I'm not sure," Will said, and I saw Sosi, under the table, slap his pant leg. "Actually, I think I might be staying out there, near school. Sosh already signed up to do research for one of her professors. I might be able to get a job like that myself. So we might get a place together, or something–we're not sure yet."

I felt Grettie look at me before I saw her do it. Her look was what I was concentrating on, instead of what Will had just said. Twenty minutes later as we cleared the table together, she grasped my wrist as I set down a stack of plates on the counter and said quietly, "You haven't talked to him yet, have you?"

"I haven't had a chance. We haven't been alone except for when she was in the shower, and there wasn't enough time."

She made a sound with her lips that I've gotten used to, over the years–a kind of pucker-smack, meaning that she understands why I'm saying or doing something, even as she thinks I shouldn't be. "You need to, Bert. He'll probably want to ... be here, this summer."

"I know." I said this, but did I really know it? I hadn't even started the treatments yet. Grettie and I both understood it was a long shot, the treatments working this time around, and yet–as Will had put it–a long shot is still a shot. And doctors make mistakes; I saw them all the time in the files I coded. I picked up a fork from one of the plates and began moving the dinner remnants into the center, only slightly aware that the action served no purpose at all. "It didn't sound as if they'd actually made plans already, did it? I think they're just tossing the idea around. And anyway, there's a long time between now and then—anything could happen. They could break up. Or ..." But I couldn't bring myself to say that maybe I wasn't going to die, after all. I tried not to say things like that.

"Bert." Grettie made the sound again, but she was standing at the dishwasher with her back to me and I only barely heard it. We rinsed and loaded in silence for a minute or two, after which she might also have felt like crying, because she changed the subject. "I know it's a cliché for us to be the ones cleaning up, but we know why we're doing it, right? It's not because we're women. It's because we know that if we do it, it'll get done right."

"And because," I said, and in unison we shouted, "It's tradition!" The smiles we gave each other then spoke so much, more than I can bear now to recall. For the three Thanksgivings that we lived together while I was in college and she was in grad school—before she met Jack, and before Friendsgiving was a thing—we hosted a holiday dinner for anyone who didn't have any other plans. It was potluck and we always ended up with more desserts than dinner food, but nobody cared. We ate and drank with friends and strangers, hiked up Mount Greylock, came back to eat and drink more, then danced all night until the police came or the last one standing had finally collapsed. The next morning we had leftovers for breakfast before we all said good-bye, and then Grettie and I split the cleaning-up duties, as we were doing now.

"Hey, keep it down in there," Cam called to us from the dining room. "You're mothers. You're supposed to be working when you're in the kitchen, not having fun."

Grettie and I wince-laughed together. I started to return to the rest of the party, but she caught my arm again. "Maybe you and Will can take a walk together later. Just the two of you."

"I doubt it. He's not going to spend any time with me if he can spend it with her."

"Not even if you tell him it's important?" When I didn't answer, she sighed and reached up to brush a piece of hair away from my eyes. It was everything I could do not to cry out and crumble into her arms. "Listen, do you want me to tell him? I am his godmother, after all. Would that be easier for you?"

I shook my head, but I couldn't speak an answer. She drew me into a hug and I wanted to stay in the feeling of it, in the scent of her skin and lips and hair, but I knew I couldn't, so I forced myself to step out of the hug and we rejoined the others at the table.

After dessert, Jack said as he did every year that it was time to go outside and walk off the bird. We went for our traditional post-Thanksgiving ramble through the part of the woods that hadn't been razed yet for the new development. I tried not to think that it would probably be my last one. Secretly, I hoped that Trudy Foote and the others fighting the developer would win, so there'd always be a place for Grettie to walk and think of me.

Maybe Sosi would stay in the picture and maybe she wouldn't. It wasn't for me to say. I just wanted my son to be happy, that's all. That's all I want.

Grettie sent us home with lots of leftovers, as she always did. I tried not to notice Bella's tearfulness when she kissed me good-bye, or the way Cam made a point of looking directly into my eyes when he said, "I'm so glad to see you, Burp"—he'd never given up his childhood name for me—before having to clear his throat. Sosi fell asleep in the car on the way home, even though it was only a ten-minute drive. In the rearview, I saw her lean her head against Will's shoulder. He reached around with the other arm to close her in. I suppose I could have said something to him then, but it wasn't the right time. And who knew how lightly she might be sleeping?

I had thought that telling Will about the cancer returning would make me feel less alone in what was happening to me. But watching him pull Sosi snug to his chest, I saw that they were a closed system. I understood: between them, they could identify only one of their four biological parents. Of course that must have been fertile soil for the seeds of their attachment. I was happy for him, but it made me feel all the more acutely that I was on the outside looking in. I realized that whenever I did tell him about the recurrence, it probably wouldn't bring me the relief I'd hoped for.

At home, helping me put the food away while he was in his room, Sosi murmured, "You love Grettie, don't you?"

I wondered if she noticed that my hands jumped a little as they placed the foil wraps in the fridge. "Of course I love her. She's my best friend. And Will's godmother." It was all I could do not to take one of those hands and press it against my chest, because of the flutter I felt there. But I wouldn't have wanted Sosi to see this—it would have given her information I didn't want her, of all people, to have.

"No, I don't mean just that." She shook that red hair of hers. "Not like a friend. You love her, I think. That's what it looks like to me."

Was she trembling inside when she said this? I couldn't tell if it intimidated her in any way, to assert such a thing to the mother of her boyfriend. How was she so confident of herself, so young? Or was it just that the wine had given her courage?

Doing my best to keep my voice steady I told her, "I'm not sure why you're saying these things to me."

She gave an expression I interpreted as a smirk, until I saw that it was not mean. "Does he know?" she asked, as she nodded in the direction of Will's room. "Does *she?*"

Thank goodness Will came out of the bedroom then, and asked what all the whispering was about. "Girl talk," Sosi said, shrugging, leading me to feel reassured (though how could I be sure?) that she wouldn't mention her suspicions to him.

Couldn't she have asked me something else, like what Will had been like as a child, or where I had grown up, or whether I liked my job? But no. "You love Grettie, don't you?" No one, not even Grettie, had understood me so well after so little time.

The next morning, maybe because I'd had a chance to sleep on it, I felt bad about the resentment I held toward Sosi. Yes, she'd asked me those questions about Grettie, but wasn't she right, after all? Maybe she just wasn't used to drinking so much wine.

And didn't it—shouldn't it—mean something that Will loved her? Even if she and I weren't immediately attracted to each other as people, she was obviously important to his life. It would only benefit us all if I could at least act like a bigger person than I felt like being, and at least pretend to warm up to her more than I had.

So at breakfast, I asked if she wanted to do a little Black Friday shopping with me, "just us girls." I saw her stiffen slightly at the word "girls," though of course she had used it herself the night before. Then in the next moment I saw her decide to let it go.

Was I also thinking that she might, like me, have been brought up by a mother who sought out sales and discounts and deals whenever possible? Maybe. It occurred to me that part of the negative feeling I had about her might be nothing more or less than a familiarity with the way I assumed she had grown up, which was the same way *I'd* grown up, and not my favorite thing to remember.

Sosi accepted my invitation and thanked me, which made me feel better; I'd already started regretting my offer. Will said he'd stay home and go through the garage to see if there were old things of his that could be donated or thrown away. It was something I'd asked him to do before he left for college in the summer, but the task got lost in the fight we had back then. When he said he'd do it now, while Sosi and I were out together, I let myself feel hopeful that it meant he might be willing to forgive me and make up. Or at least start talking to me again—if not the way he used to, then at least something close.

As we drove to my preferred shopping center, not the fancy plaza with all the boutiques but the one with the chain stores near the highway, Sosi said, "You haven't always lived here, have you." It had the air of a challenge rather than a question, but I was determined not to rise to her bait.

Or maybe she was just seeking kinship with me, since we both came from towns much poorer than this one? It felt better to make the more generous assumption. I wondered if Will had told her my background, or if she just recognized it in me.

"No. I lived in an apartment in Allston before I had Will. They called it the student ghetto." Sosi cringed a little, and I realized you probably weren't supposed to say ghetto anymore. I decided not to acknowledge the cringe. "But I thought it would be better to bring up a kid out here."

"Why?"

I figured she had to know the answer—she just wanted to make me say it. Admit to my own snobbishness. Well, I wasn't embarrassed about the choices I'd made for my son. "Better schools, for one. More space." Then, because I knew she was thinking it, I robbed her of the chance to ask. "Mainly, we live here because of Grettie. I knew I'd need help if I was going to be a single mother." Even as I said those last words, I thought *No, no no!* understanding only then, instinctively, that Sosi would take this as another invitation, this time to pursue the subject of my single motherhood.

She stuck her nose up to the crack to breathe deep, as if, in the absence of the wine available the day before, she sought the nerve she needed from the atmosphere instead. "Listen, I probably shouldn't do this, but I wanted to ask you something. Will keeps saying you won't talk to him about it—his father. He said you promised to tell him when he turned eighteen, but then you backed out."

For the first time—because I was looking at her more closely than I had before, focusing on what I saw rather than what I heard—I noticed all the freckles she had on her face. Cute, really. She probably didn't think so, but it wasn't the kind of thing I could ask. "I didn't promise him that, Sosh." His nickname for her slipped out, and she frowned a little. "Sorry. *Sosi.* I'm not saying he was lying—I'm saying he misunderstood. He misunderstood for all that time, all his life, so of course it upset him when I couldn't give him what he thought he was going to get."

He and I had had the conversation—was it fair to call it that, instead of a fight? *Fight* was more like it—in August, a week or so before he left to go to school. We had three things to celebrate last summer: his graduation from high school; the year's anniversary of my surgery, which we believed had cured my cancer; and, in August, his big birthday. Though part of me dreaded living alone again, as I had before he was born, I was also excited for him. So I felt pretty upbeat when he and I went to dinner, at his favorite sushi restaurant, on the night of his birthday. The air conditioning was on full blast, and because I'd lost a few pounds during my illness and treatment that I hadn't gained back yet, I couldn't stay warm even though I'd brought a sweater. But I did my best not to shiver, to conceal my chill from him.

"I'm so glad you're all better," he said, looking shyly at his plate as if he were afraid he might not be doing the right thing by telling me this. "I can't tell you how scared I was, when you were going through all that."

"When we were going through it," I said, reaching to put my hand over his. "I don't mind telling you I was scared, too. But everything's good, now. Right?"

He started to nod, then stopped abruptly and cleared his throat. "Actually," he said, and I steeled myself, intuiting suddenly what was to come. "I wanted to ask you something. I guess my birthday being now, in August, means I was conceived in December, right? Like, around Christmas?"

From out of nowhere came the smell of peppermint mocha, and I almost gagged on the food in my throat. Then I tried to change the subject, but Will was on to me. "Mom, I'm eighteen now. You told me I'd find out when I was eighteen. I have a right to know who my father is."

It wasn't exactly true, that I had told him that. I might

have let him believe that I'd tell him. But I'm sure I never said it outright.

"Honey. I've told you a million times, I can't say."

Of course he must have been expecting this, but he remained undeterred. If it hadn't been for what we were talking about, I would have told him I admired his persistence. His *grit*—I think that's the new word.

"Just give me *something*," he begged. I'd never heard quite such a desperate tone in his voice, even when the emetophobia was at its worst. I thought he might be about to cry.

If only I could have told him—and made him believe—that it's for his own sake, not mine. That it's not myself or an anonymous donor I'm protecting.

Was I tempted to give him the name of the cryobank I'd researched back then? Of course I was. Anything to stop the questions.

But it was too risky. Instead I only told him I could see, from how upset he was, that I'd made a mistake in deciding to use a donor who preferred not to be identified. But at the time, I said, I thought it was the right decision.

"Well, it wasn't." Will blew air through his lips, the sound he makes when he's dismissing something I've said. "Can't you understand why I'd want information about the other half of my genes?"

"Knowing everything about where you come from isn't all it's cracked up to be," I said, more sharply than I'd intended. "And a lot of fathers aren't so great."

He sat back and shook his head—just a little shake,

but it was enough to make me catch my breath. "The only person who could say something like that, and not realize how it sounds," he said, overenunciating even though I'd told him what an annoying habit it was, "is a person who *knows*." Then he must have registered my reaction, and concluded that if he had any hope of persuading me, he had to back off. He made an obvious effort to smile. "I promise I can handle whatever I might find out. Like if the guy turns out to be a drug addict or something. Or a Republican." He let the smile grow, but when I didn't respond, it faded and he tried another tack. "You know I'm going to find him someday. Somehow. So you may as well tell me now."

I *didn't* know or believe this, but there seemed no point in telling him so. Needless to say, the dinner ended on a much worse note than it started on. For the week between then and the day I drove him to school, it's not as if we didn't speak to each other, but it wasn't the same as it had been, especially during the time I was sick. It took everything in me not to start crying until I left his dorm building, which I ended up having to lean against because I was doubled over with the pain of it. Groups of other new students and parents walked by me and some mother called out gently, "I know how you feel."

But of course, she didn't–not really. At her side was her son's father, toting an electronics box on his shoulder. Another mother approached and asked if I needed help, and forcing myself to stand up straight and suck the tears in, I told her No, I just needed to get back to my car. She patted me on the shoulder, reached into her purse, and handed me a ribboned cellophane bag of homemade cookies. "You need these more than she does," she told me, nodding at the cheerful daughter beside her, who smiled and wished me luck.

I thought Will might call me, homesick, once I left campus and drove back home (shoving the cookies in my mouth as fast as I could chew and swallow, hoping the gluttony of it would make me feel punished—it did). But not only did I never receive such a call, he sent me an email after he'd been there a week, telling me that he thought it might be best for both of us if we "took a break" from each other. He needed to test himself, he wrote. It had been just him and me for so long, he realized now that he'd depended too much on me, it was time for him to see what it felt like to be on his own. He ended by asking if I would please not call or text or respond to this note.

"Best for both of us"? No. You can imagine what went through me, when I read those words. You can imagine that my impulse was to call him right up and say, *Don't do this. Okay? Please don't do this. All right, I'll tell you what you want to know.*

The truth is that I'd always intended to tell him, in the far-off "someday". I understood that he had a right. I just wanted to launch him, first—that's the phrase I hear my friends using, when they talk about seeing their kids into adulthood and the world. Given Will's nervous history, I decided it was better to wait.

I hadn't figured—who would?—on running out of time. How could I tell him the truth about where he came from when he still didn't know this other, more immediate thing, which was that the cancer had come back, and I was running out of time?

Besides, if he meant what he'd said, his asking for a "break" was unrelated to my disappointing him by withholding information he believed would help him find his father.

I had my doubts it was unrelated, though. Who am I kidding—of course it was related.

I was not invited to his school for Family Weekend, and he did not return for a visit all through September and October, and for half of November. The day he texted to say he wanted to come home for Thanksgiving and bring his girlfriend, I responded within a minute *Yes! Can't wait!* and like a pathetic schoolgirl with a crush hanging onto a scrap of hope tossed to her by the quarterback, I read his text over and over, allowing myself to feel grateful that he'd used the word "home."

Sitting next to me in the parked car at the shopping center, Sosi picked at a hangnail, no doubt to give her something besides me to look at. "I know I said I didn't care about finding my birth parents. The chances that they're not people I'd ever want to know, considering where I come from, are pretty good." She yanked the piece of skin off, then had to put her finger in her mouth when it bled. Speaking around it she mumbled, "But Will's a different story. Sperm donors generally have their lives together, right? They're vetted and everything. So, I just don't understand."

"I'm not sure what more I can say," I told her, looking not at her but straight ahead through the windshield. "Other than what I've said already, which is that I don't have any information that would be helpful to him."

This was the truth. It was a good way to put it, I thought.

But she went on as if I hadn't spoken at all. "I can tell this is hard for you. And I wouldn't be asking if I didn't think you were the only way he might find anything out. There're no guarantees with those DNA kits, he knows it probably wouldn't lead to his ... paternity." I appreciated the sensitivity it showed, for her to use this word instead of *father*. But I wasn't about to tell her so.

She took her finger out of her mouth to check it, but the blood hadn't stopped. "To be honest, I think if he ever does do one, it won't be for a while. He knows the results would probably just disappoint him. And he has enough on his plate right now, with school and everything."

I couldn't tell if she paused before *and everything*, as if to emphasize the *everything* without defining it. But she might have. As much as I hate the expression about people having enough or too much on their plates, I felt relieved to hear that Will hadn't sent off a swab yet and might not be doing so anytime soon. In the next moment the relief vanished when Sosi said, with a gentleness that threw me off, "Is there some reason you think he might have something to be afraid of?"

What was it with this girl and her intuitions? I stayed very still and took my time before answering, fully aware that whatever I said would get reported back to him. I began with "I wouldn't know." Then, despite realizing it was risky, I said, "This isn't something I want to talk to you about." In an effort to reduce the sting I added, "I appreciate your interest" (though I didn't), "but this is really between him and me."

I watched her mind fill up with all the things she might say to me. She had some more words planned, I could tell. But in the end, she only told me she didn't feel like shopping, after all. I realized I was exhausted, myself, even though it wasn't even ten in the morning. I started the car and we headed home.

Though we'd been gone no more than half an hour, when we returned to the house I saw that Will had piled a dozen open boxes of his stuff on the curb. Old games and toys; stuffed animals; the file containing his art projects, essays, tests, class photographs, and report cards from elementary through high school; tennis rackets, T-ball mitt and bat; participation ribbons from the field-day events he'd been forced to enter in middle school—all of this I took in at a glance, understanding that he hadn't even sorted through the boxes for anything he might wish to save. Balanced at the top of one (and I couldn't help thinking he'd placed it there on purpose, so I wouldn't miss it) was Chutes and Ladders, the box faded and battered from so much use. That was a phew! His entire childhood sat outside the house, waiting to be picked up with the trash.

Sosi went inside, while I stood there too stunned to follow. After a few minutes I heard a door open and braced myself for the approach of either Will or Sosi, but instead it was my neighbor Pascal, emerging from her own house next door. "You okay?" she asked gently, and I realized she must have observed Will toting out all his stuff, each item adding to the accumulation of the pain she knew I'd feel when I saw it.

"Hmm," I said, hoping it sounded like a yes, but knowing it didn't. Pascal touched my shoulder, but I jerked away.

"Okay," she said, after a moment. In a low voice before she retreated back to her own space she added, "If it makes any difference, it hurts me to see it, too."

I murmured and turned to step back toward my house. Inside I found Will sitting at my desk in the corner of the living room, where he had my computer open and appeared to be scrolling through files.

I was so perplexed that although my brain yelled *Stop!* I could not form the word with my voice. All I could think was that he had opened my account on the health portal and learned about my recurrence, before I could tell him about it myself.

But he did not look upset, so I thought maybe I was wrong. My relief didn't last long, though, because as he clicked away and I moved closer, I saw that he had entered not my own record but the coding system of the hospital I worked for, which of course is highly confidential and restricted by multiple passwords—which, of course, I had never given to Will. "What are you doing?" This I managed to get out, though barely. "How did you get into that?" I wasn't even sure he'd heard me until he finally looked up and said, with a smugness that might have been bravado or might have been real (I was dismayed not to be able to tell which), "Uncle Hal taught me some things."

I lowered myself onto the couch, feeling for it first with my hands to make sure it was solid beneath me. Sosi took a seat, also cautiously, on the other end. "You can't do that," I told him. "You're not supposed to be in there."

"Yeah, well. A lot of things aren't supposed to happen." He picked up the pad he'd been scribbling on. "So: Celia Santoro? Heart problems, possibly exacerbated by cocaine use. It wouldn't be good if the hospital found out you were sharing confidential medical files with people who aren't supposed to see them, would it, Mom?"

I heard my voice wobble as I asked him, "What are you talking about?" Of course I recognized that he was referring to the file of patient 1998207. But I had never seen her actual name. "What do you mean, *Celia Santoro?*"

His shrug looked wobbly, too. But he lifted his chin and tried to bluff his way through. "Like I said. Uncle Hal taught me some things."

Sosi gasped. It was as if she made the sound for both of us. And when he heard it, Will started in his seat as if she had just called him back to consciousness, woken him up. He looked at the screen in front of him, then immediately reached to close the file. I saw that his hand was trembling. "You don't mean that," Sosi told him, though by now it was obvious to us all that he'd already come to his senses. "Apologize," she added in an urgent whisper, and I was as shocked by that—and by the fact that he obeyed her—as by the offense she ordered him to apologize for.

In fact, he couldn't *stop* apologizing. I told him it was all right, though of course it wasn't. He said he'd never intended to force me, by threatening to disclose those medical secrets, into giving me the information he wanted; he'd opened the computer planning only to look around, to see if there was anything obvious on my desktop that might be a clue. Please, would I forgive him? I said yes, but then I couldn't help summarizing back to him what he'd just said: "So, you only meant to spy. Not hack into a system you're not allowed access to. Not blackmail me."

He winced. "I didn't think of it as any of those things."

Even now, even though I know better, I'm tempted to believe that he's stayed away from me all this time because he feels so guilty about what he did that day, that's how upset he looked.

I probably don't need to say that during the rest of our time together, no one spoke much. I had to lie down on my bed for a while, while Will and Sosi did schoolwork in front of the TV. For dinner, we ate turkey leftovers and the faux fettuccini Alfredo I'd made for their arrival. Originally they'd planned to stay until Sunday, but instead, the next morning at breakfast, they said they thought they'd head back to campus. I didn't mind; I was weary of the visit, something I never thought I'd say about my son.

Only one more time were Sosi and I alone, when Will went to fill up the gas tank while she packed. "He told me the ipecac story, you know," she said. Was she making it a point to fold that lacy nightgown right in front of me, and take far longer to do so than the action required? "Maybe I shouldn't say this, but you do know that that could be considered child abuse, don't you?"

I'd stopped being taken aback by the things she said to me. Well, not really. But it had stopped being such a surprise.

"That's not your business," I said, but I was wrong, because Will had made it her business. After they left I watched until the car had pulled away from the house, and gave it enough time to reach the end of the street before I went to the curb and lugged all of the boxes he'd tried to get rid of back into the garage.

It really didn't take all that much longer, using the back route instead of the highway, to get from the hospital to Grettie's house. Despite her assurances about when the garbage and recycling trucks always picked up, the barrel and bins remained full where they'd been placed at the curb. I swore and parked in the driveway. I hadn't considered this possibility. Should I wait? And if so, for how long? The appointment with the therapist was for three o'clock. It was one-forty-five now. If I did wait, it could only be for half an hour, and that would be cutting it close.

Or should I leave now and come back later? I couldn't decide. I'd really wanted to have this chore over with by the time I saw him, so that after our appointment, I didn't have to worry about anything other than getting home. I swore again and stepped out of the car, feeling hot and a little dizzy. The temp must have gone even higher than what the weather people had said.

"Roberta!" Almost immediately I was approached by a woman in her mid-forties with a severely angled cut to her obviously dyed black hair. This was Grettie's next-door neighbor, Trudy Foote. She and her husband are the ones who started the fight in the neighborhood over Arcadia Glen, the subdivision a developer started building last year on the dozen acres of woods at the end of this street. Trudy organized the opposition—circulating petitions, speaking out at Town Meeting, getting people to post signs on their lawns—even before the first six houses went up. Then the developer's backhoe struck a skull fragment, and it was discovered that the lot contained several unmarked graves, which the previous landowner had not disclosed and swore he'd never known about.

After that, the protests got even louder, especially when a local archivist surmised that one of the buried bodies belonged to a Civil War veteran who'd had a hand in founding the town. Now, instead of objecting only to the destruction of the woods, crowded classrooms, and an overloaded water supply, Trudy and the other opponents have added "desecration of our history" to the list of things we would suffer if Arcadia Glen went forward.

Bullshit, Grettie says. She believes their real problem is with the affordable housing the developer included in his plans in order to get the permit he needed from the town. "They just don't want 'affordable' kids in their kids' classrooms," she declared when all of it started, on a night last fall when I invited myself over because I hadn't talked to Will in the three weeks since he'd gone away to college, and I could feel the walls closing in. "They think it'll lower their property values and the school ratings, end up ruining their kids' lives. I'm sure they love affordable housing in theory—as long as it's built somewhere else."

Everything's up in the air right now with Arcadia Glen. Work on the remaining six houses has been halted while the developer tries to figure out if he can legally relocate the graves. Grettie and Jack think he should be allowed to do so, and to finish the construction. That night Grettie told me, "You of all people should understand why this is important, Bert."

Me "of all people"? It wasn't often—hardly ever, in all the years we'd known each other, and it always seemed accidental, to the point that she seemed contrite after-ward—that Grettie referred even in passing to the eco-nomic differences that had always existed between us. But she's right, it's true that I wouldn't be living out here myself, in the rare rental on the edge of the town next to hers, if a different developer hadn't been given the go-ahead the year before I gave birth to Will.

But instead of responding directly, I told Grettie, "I can understand not wanting to lose the woods." We've been walking our dogs there together for years. All I have to say to Scout is "Ready for your walk?" and he lumbers past me to wait, panting and scrabbling, at the door.

"Well, of course, I can understand that, too." Gret-tie opened a bottle of wine, but I declined. I was too depressed, it was too dangerous. She poured herself a glass. "If I thought saving the woods was the real reason for their hysteria, I'd have more sympathy."

Her indignation had been ignited afresh by a neigh-borhood email thread Trudy Foote started when it looked as if there might be a way to make the developer back down. "Please join us in the effort to prevent the further rape of our beloved woodlands," she'd written. "They are an oasis of tranquility in this stressful, demanding world. There's a reason we all love living here—we want to be far from the maddening crowd."

"*Maddening* crowd!" Grettie slapped the kitchen table as she recited the message, which she obviously knew by heart. "Maddening crowd, do you believe that? And really, using the word 'woodlands'—as if we're all letting our dogs shit on dryads and nymphs."

I laughed, even though I didn't know what a dryad was. It was one of the reasons I loved her, how Grettie got about things like that. I mean *love*, not loved. *Gets*, not got.

I'd thought she was going to say "And really, using the word 'rape'," because that was the one that caught my attention, it seemed too dramatic for what was actually going on.

I made my murmuring noise. The truth, though I didn't want to say so, is that I was already hoping the protesters would win. Not so we won't have affordable housing, but because of the graves. Shouldn't a "final resting place" be exactly that? My feeling is, once something's buried, you should leave it alone.

I want to be cremated and scattered wherever Will chooses. No bones left behind by me.

Standing before me now between her own house and Grettie's, Trudy carried several plastic grocery bags that appeared weighed down with pellets of dog waste. After she called my name, I had no choice but to acknowledge that I'd heard her. I knew her, after all. Our sons were in the same grade, and before the war over Arcadia Glen, I used to see her every year at Grettie and Jack's holiday open house. Grettie liked to say that Trudy had all the wit and charm of a corn muffin.

"Trudy! Hi!"

She moved closer, and for a moment I thought she was going to reach out and touch me. Startled, I pulled away. She said, "Listen, I heard about—I mean, I'm so sorry. Are you okay?"

"Of course I'm okay." If she was going to ask such a stupid question, she didn't deserve the real answer. "I'm just really hot, that's all." I explained my mission with the barrel and the bins.

"Don't tell me they asked you to drive all the way over here just for that?" Her expression shifted from one of concern to incredulity. "I would have been happy to take them in."

"Oh, I don't mind. I was coming over to pick something up, anyway."

"You were? What?" Although of course the question was as inappropriate as it could possibly have been, I was the one who felt panicked about answering, because it was, of course, a lie. I could not think of a single item in Grettie's house that I might have swung by to retrieve. Instead, I gestured at the plastic bags Trudy carried and said, "So, you've become a one-woman neighborhood clean-up crew?"

Trudy grimaced, ineffectually shoving her hair behind one ear with the top of the hand not holding the bags of turds. "People are so irresponsible," she said, in a tone inviting my agreement. "Not all of them, but too many. I look out my window and see them let their dogs do their business on someone's lawn, then walk away. It just makes me want to scream. Fenton thought this was a more constructive idea." She lifted the bags, and I remembered her husband (Fenton Foote—what kind of person names a child Fenton Foote?!), a short and shy-looking man who seemed ready to admit to anyone who'd listen his obsession with JonBenét Ramsey, the six-year-old beauty queen murdered on a Christmas night in her own house out in Colorado. One New Year's Day, just after the tenth anniversary of the girl's death, I spent more than half an hour listening to Fenton expound upon the case. "The intruder theory makes sense because what are we supposed to believe? It was just a coincidence that JonBenét happened to be a Little Miss pageant queen? No. It could have been some pervert who broke in while the family was out celebrating the holiday with their friends, stayed hidden when they came home, then woke the kid up after everybody else had fallen asleep. Did you know she told two people—one of her friends, and the friend's mother—that Santa told her he was going to visit her in secret on Christmas night?" Asking me this, Fenton's blue eyes had widened, as if his own question had only just then reminded him of this disturbing and possibly pertinent detail of the famous crime. I shook my head and told him *No, I hadn't heard that.* Part of me wanted to escape the conversation, but another part was fascinated by the fact that Fenton was so fascinated. "But it's equally plausible—probably even more so—that it was somebody in the family who did it. The mother or the brother. When the police came in the morning, Patsy Ramsey had on full makeup and the same clothes as the day before. And the brother's penknife was found right next to the body. Not to mention that the father headed straight for that hidden room in the basement, where the body was, when the policewoman told him to start searching the house. And he said, 'Oh, my God, there she is,' even before he turned on the light." Fenton took a sip of Grettie's famous hot buttered rum as he allowed me to imagine the scene.

"The saddest thing about it, JonBenét had a red heart drawn on one of her palms," he continued. "Most people think it was the mother who killed her. And that her husband helped cover it up."

"Mothers don't kill their children," I told him. "Not unless they're insane, like that one who drove her kids into the ocean. Or the one who drowned her kids in a tub. Or like Gretchen in *Faust*." I was really proud of myself for that literary one, it occurred to me at the last second, but I don't think Fenton noticed because he started talking again before I was done.

"They didn't think she did it on purpose." At least he seemed willing to concede my point about mothers, as he prepared to make one of his own. "They thought it was an accident, like maybe she just lost it when JonBenét wet the bed or something. There were lots of things that pointed to Patsy. They couldn't exclude her as having written the ransom note, and one of the cops said that when she was supposedly wailing in grief after the body was found, with her hands over her face, what she was really doing was watching the cop between the slits of her fingers." He raised his own index finger toward me and made a Gotcha sound, at which point, finally, I said,

"Mothers don't hurt their children" before excusing my-self.

Trudy and Fenton were the parents of Derek, who'd been friends with Will in school until eighth grade, when Trudy decided to take Derek out and teach him at home. The boys had originally met in the nurse's office of the elementary school. Derek had food allergies and Will had asthma, so they overlapped on visits to the nurse. Then there were the tennis lessons they took together. More than a few times, I'd done the favor of picking up Derek and shuttling him to Apex and then back home, because that was the year Trudy had some mysterious illness or syndrome that never got diagnosed. Grettie started out having sympathy for her, but as time went by and Trudy could supply no name for her disease, Grettie expressed suspicion that it was just one of those "fatigue disorders," suggesting through her tone of voice that she did not have the patience for or a belief in such things.

Derek and Will spent a fair amount of time together, but that was when they were little. When Derek didn't start high school with the rest of his class, the boys lost touch. A year ago, Will suspected Derek of being the one to call in the bomb scare before commencement. As a home-schooled kid in the district he was allowed to graduate with Will and the other seniors, but Will's guess was that the prospect embarrassed him too much, because he wasn't really a member of the class. "His mother would never have let him skip the ceremony," Will said to me, "so he had to come up with some other way to get out of it. I'd bet good money on it being him."

Though I'd never held anything against Derek before, I grew angry hearing Will explain his theory. I'd been very excited about graduation, not only for the usual reasons, but because, as the class's salutatorian, Will was scheduled to speak from the podium. At first, he told me he intended to decline—they could let the Number Three person go up and give a speech, he said, after the valedictorian gave hers. When he saw how disappointed I was, he said he'd think about it. Shortly afterward he told me he'd changed his mind, but only on the condition that I didn't ask to see the speech beforehand. He didn't want help, and he wanted it to be a surprise. I said of course, whatever would make him the most comfortable. I was thrilled that he decided to go ahead with it, especially considering that in the past, any kind of attention like that would have been unthinkable because of the emetophobia. And he'd worked so hard, so hard to get the grades he did, it was nice to think he'd be recognized for that. I couldn't wait to see him be honored—I was so proud of him. Needless to say, I was devastated when the news about the bomb threat came and they canceled commencement.

A week later there was a makeup ceremony, but Will didn't want to go. He said a lot of kids had already left for summer vacation and wouldn't be there; "You'd be bummed, Mom," he told me, "it would be totally lame."

"No, I wouldn't," I said, but I couldn't dissuade him.

Would he read the speech to me, then? I asked. He seemed to consider it briefly, then shook his head, saying the moment had passed.

Derek Foote had stolen that moment from me. Standing in front of me now, his mother appeared to have recovered from whatever disorder she suffered back when our sons were young. When I could see that she was generating some other question I would not want to answer, I headed it off by asking one of my own. "How's Derek? At ...?" It was acceptable, I knew, to forget the name of the college attended by an acquaintance's son. Given how little I saw of him anymore, I gave myself bonus points for remembering her kid's name.

"Oh." It took her longer than it would have taken most people to switch gears. She lowered her face as she gave a final twist to the plastic bags dangling from her wrist. "He's fine. He's actually living at home now, taking some online classes—it gives him more options, in the long run. The wave of the future, I guess. Online. And yours?"

It was not lost on me that what Trudy was essentially saying was that her kid had dropped out of real school, and that she, like the tennis pro, had forgotten Will's name. I know I should not consider conversations with other mothers to be competitions, but I couldn't help thinking *I win.*

I told her Will was majoring in neuroscience (I admit that sounded more impressive than "psychology" to me, and he *had* used that word—he wanted to study the connection between the brain and the body), and that he had a beautiful girlfriend he'd brought home for Thanksgiving. I could have added that I had not seen him in more than six months—six months! How was that possible?—

but of course I did not.

I sensed that Trudy was struggling, trying to decide whether to say what was next on her mind. I waited. "Listen, Roberta, if you happen to see Derek around anywhere, will you let me know?"

A quick shot of apprehension spiked through me. "Why? Is he missing?"

"Oh, no. Nothing like that." She gave an obviously forced laugh. "I just need him to do something. Just—if you happen to see him."

I said Sure automatically before adding, "I'd better go in and get it," all too aware that I had still failed to identify the it. She watched me as I fitted my key into Grettie and Jack's door. From their stoop, I watched *her* as she walked slowly back toward her own porch, then— instead of dumping the bags of poop into her own barrel, as I expected—carried them up the steps toward her house.

It would have disgusted Will so much, to see those bags she was carrying. Dog poop was one of the things that set his stomach on edge. When we walked Scout together, he had to turn his back while I gathered the turds in a bag—I used the opaque bags the Sunday *Globe* came in, so he wouldn't be able to see through to what was inside. At one point I'd tried to persuade him that it would be good for him to muster the strength of mind to clean up after Scout himself, not because I minded doing it, but because it was better to face the things that make us nervous. Get over them, manage our fear. And to his credit, he tried—once, before he began gagging and then retched at the side of the street. After that, I stopped pestering him about it. He'd grow out of this phase, I remember thinking—the weak stomach, the sensitive nerves. Of course, he didn't grow out of it, he got worse. It was my fault for not forcing him to keep at it, to do a little more each day until the sight and smell of a dog's turd didn't have that kind of power over him.

But by the time I found it in myself to encourage him to try again, it was too late.

Dear Sosi, went the letter I wrote in my head, which of course I would never send. It's not "the ipecac story." It's the story of how I tried to save my son from something that might have killed him.

If that sounds dramatic, I'm sorry. But I know all too well—it's one of the things from my own past I'd like to forget, but I can't, I know because I've tried—how dangerous a place your own mind can be. Some poet, I'm pretty sure it was Milton, said the mind can make a heaven of hell, or a hell of heaven. I think about that a lot. I'm pretty sure my life wasn't a heaven when my mind felt like hell, but the point is that it's hard to get yourself out of that danger sometimes; you need someone else to help.

He'd always had the weak stomach. Got carsick over the smallest bumps. Dog poop wasn't the only thing that made him retch; it could be the smell of fish or mayonnaise, the sight of sausage or cheese. In fifth grade his class dissected fetal pigs, and even though I thought it would be better if he went to school and proved to himself that he could conquer his dread, I let him stay home that day. This decision might have been the worst one, the one that allowed it to snowball after that—his emetophobia.

For him, a fear of doing it in public, especially in front of people he knew. When I asked him, he said he couldn't imagine anything worse happening to him. People looking, pointing, laughing—making revolted faces. "But it's a natural bodily function," I told him. "Everyone does it. It's nothing to be ashamed of." I tried to reassure him with my background as a medical professional.

"Try to think of yourself as a biological organism," I advised further. "Like, think of a snail. You don't think they're embarrassed to trail slime behind them, do you?" Too late, I realized this wasn't a good example; hearing *slime* made him feel sick all over again, I could tell.

When he got through shuddering he said, "Are you telling me feelings aren't real?"

"Well, of course they are." I wasn't exactly sure what he meant.

It used to be, when he was little, he'd look in my eyes when I told him something, and I saw that it had entered his head and heart. There was a little dent over one of his eyebrows that pulsed with how hard he was listening. He believed me, then. What I said to him mattered.

When he was older and I tried to persuade him that throwing up was not a big deal, even if it happened in front of other people, I could tell that he barely heard my words before he rejected them. Though he'd always had the weak stomach, it took hold of him—this fear—during his first semester of sixth grade. He was sitting in World

History, listening to the lesson about Hiroshima, when all of a sudden he felt the moment of panic that signals imminent vomiting. He left the classroom, and once he was out in the hallway, the nausea passed. But instead of going back in, he went to the school nurse, who called me to pick him up. That was the beginning of it, I think. The beginning of the grip it had on him. Though he was not physically sick, the next day he was afraid to go back to World History, and within a week he was afraid to go to school at all.

Maybe it was the idea of the bombing that did it, I suggested. Hiroshima had been a terrible thing.

He shook his head and told me it was more than that. He said he was pretty sure he needed therapy. Could I take him to see someone?

I tried not to show any reaction when he said the word *therapy*.

"Let's not jump right to that," I said. "If it ends up being absolutely necessary—if there's no other solution— then sure. But let's try some other things first. What about if you said to yourself 'I'm feeling a little nervous, but I know there's not actually anything to be afraid of.' Do you think that could work?"

The look on his face and the sound he made between his lips were enough of an answer: *You've got to be kidding.*

"Then how about medication?" I asked. "There are some good anti-anxiety meds, I could ask my friends at the hospital." It's a measure of how much I didn't want him to see a therapist that I jumped straight to the idea of drugs.

I know this was wrong. I knew it then. But I can't change what happened. It was the best I could do.

He did not want to try medication. First of all, he worried the pills would upset his stomach, which would defeat the purpose of taking them. But he said it also went against everything he believed in, everything he was learning from tai chi. He wanted to rely solely on his mind for this, he told me: it was a psychological problem, not a physical one.

"There's a reason you named me Will," he reminded me, smiling grimly. I smiled back; it was a joke between us. Well, not a joke, but a routine. An exchange we'd been having ever since he was old enough to understand that *will* was a noun as well as a name. He often got asked what his real name was—William, or Willard, or even Wilhelm—but I told him it wasn't short for anything, I'd decided on just *Will* because I wanted him to embody it, I wanted him to have a will that nobody else would ever be able to bend or break.

I also wanted him to have a name that meant something to him, a name that was his alone. My sister and I were named after our mother's father and husband, Robert and Stephen. It's hard to feel that your name belongs to you when it's just a variation of somebody else's.

And I figured it was a simple, solid name, one that wouldn't cause him any grief, any stupid nicknames. In fourth grade some joker, some new girl too precocious for her own good, said to him, "Will Chase? What will you chase, Will? You Will chase what?"—but that was about it.

I was proud of him when he said he wanted to use his Will Power (yes, I'm afraid we did call it that) to solve his stomach problem, even as I worried that willpower would not be enough.

Maybe he saw this doubt on my face. "Where do you think this comes from?" he asked me. "Is this what Grandma had?"

He had never met my mother because she died before he was born, but he'd always referred to her as "Grandma." It made me sad, first because they'd never know each other, and second because I guessed that using the intimate nickname allowed him to pretend he had more family than he actually did. I know how jealous he'd always felt when he heard his classmates refer to their grandmas and grandpas. Almost as jealous as when he heard them say Dad.

"No," I told him. "What Grandma had was depression." And alcoholism, I thought, but didn't say—why pile on with a fact irrelevant to his own suffering? "This is something else, a form of anxiety. If we can figure out how to help you feel less anxious, the fear of throwing up should go away."

"That's why I thought maybe a therapist," he said.

"What about that poster in your bedroom?" I was grasping at straws now, but (I wished mightily) maybe he wouldn't realize. *"Yield and overcome—?"* He looked at me without understanding.

"Maybe you're fighting it too much. Remember what you told me when we did that exercise with the hands?

Don't try so hard, you said. Maybe it would help if instead of trying so hard to control it, you gave *up* control."

Saying this, I remembered suddenly the Saturday morning years ago, when he was a year and a half old and Cam was almost three, that Grettie and I took them to a water babies' class. We stepped into the pool carrying the boys and formed a circle with other parent-baby pairs and the instructor who led us in splashing, singing, and chasing plastic balls she skimmed across the water's surface. At one point she sat all the kids on the pool's edge and gave the parents Styrofoam noodles, instructing us to try to balance on our knees. No problem, I thought, but it was deceptively awkward. I kept slipping off the thing, and so did everyone else. The children loved watching the grown-ups topple into the water. They giggled so hard that one little girl actually fell in herself.

Don't fight it and it will be easier, the instructor called to us. I thought I had never heard such magical words in my life. The moment I stopped trying to balance, I could kneel on the noodle without any problem at all. The same was true, I saw, for Grettie and everyone else. Remember that, I told myself. Don't fight it and it will be easier.

"This is what I'm going to teach your children," the instructor said.

Will didn't want to go back for the second week. He didn't like the water, he was afraid to dunk his head. I thought about the teacher's phrase from time to time for a few days, but then it went the way of so many other things, and I forgot, until I found myself flailing in the search for a way to help Will stop being afraid of vomiting in public.

But he dismissed the suggestion. "I have to fight it," he said. "Otherwise it'll win."

I came up with another idea: what if he asked his teachers if he could sit near the classroom doors? He could tell them that he was having a claustrophobia "issue." Maybe if he believed he could get up and leave whenever he wanted—if the teachers gave him permission to do so—the fear and the nausea wouldn't be so bad.

He listened with an expression that was mostly doubt, but that also contained a hint of hope. Well, I could try it, he told me. I asked if he wanted me to write a note. No, he said—he'd take care of it himself. He was skeptical, but he came home that first day and said, "Hey, guess what, it kind of works. It's worse when I have to force myself to sit there, better when I know I have the option to escape. It makes a difference to have an out."

I knew what he was talking about, but of course I didn't tell him. An out was what the bush in the cemetery had been once, for me.

I was more relieved than I can say when he seemed to be okay for the next few years, through most of high school; after a while, with the "emergency exit" strategy in place and the relaxation he felt from his tai chi practice, the thought of puking in public hardly ever crossed his mind. I allowed myself to believe it was a phase he'd survived, something unfortunate he'd endured once but wouldn't have to go through again.

Then, when he was a senior, it came back with a vengeance. I don't use that term lightly; it really did feel as if some force had finally gotten fed up with being ignored, and decided to return and punish the person who'd done the ignoring. I know better—I know it was just part of his own mind, not an actual soul with a score to settle—but whatever the reason, it recurred worse than ever.

I can only assume it was related to my diagnosis and surgery. He'd been doing so well, and then that happened. Do I feel guilty about it? Of course, even though I guess getting cancer wasn't my fault. It caused him to falter, his nervousness came back. Not that summer, but as soon as school started, he was in trouble again.

The initial wave came over him during the first week of the semester, in an assembly on lockdown procedures and other safety protocols, when he forgot (that's how far the whole thing had receded) to make a point of sitting at the end of the long auditorium row. From the stage, the speaker was instructing them all about what to do in the case of an active shooter when all of a sudden Will felt the old, familiar urge to vomit, and the certainty that it was about to happen. He stood to make his way to the aisle and out of the room, but a teacher he didn't know, two seats away, snapped at him to sit back down. Afraid of making a scene, Will obeyed and then proceeded to suffer through the next hour, trying to do tai chi routines in his head and slow his breath, but for some reason, probably because it slowed his mind down, too, this only made things worse.

Think about what that would feel like—the moment before you know you're going to throw up, only it's not just a moment, it's ten minutes, half an hour, an hour. He managed to tolerate the sensation (which he later described to me as *agony*) for the rest of assembly, which you might think would make him feel confident that he could do the same the next time. But no, the experience took so much out of him that when he got home that day he went to bed, not coming out again for dinner or anything else, and I heard him crying. Sobbing under the sheets.

He needed help, I knew. The next day, I let him stay home. At home he was all right—he knew it didn't matter if he threw up or not, so he didn't worry about it. It was the public part he dreaded.

An idea occurred to me, springing up through a memory from my own childhood. I dismissed it at first, then fought long and hard with myself. Then decided it was worth trying, because what if it worked? I thought it might work. What if it would have worked, and I hadn't done it? I would have hated myself.

I went to the supermarket. You could buy it on the shelves at that time, only a few years ago—over the counter, even in the grocery store, in the same aisle as teething bracelets and Enfamil. Why would they let us do that if it was so bad? I mean, it comes from a plant. It was a mistake, I know that now. It's been taken off the shelves. But at the time, being able to buy it along with toilet paper and apples and the ice cream bars Will liked—it reassured me.

I do things for him, as you know (went the letter to Sosi I composed in my head but would never write). Less so than before he left home, but probably more than I should. This includes making his breakfast. The day I let him stay home, after the active-shooter assembly, was a Friday. Though he didn't say anything, I could tell he worried all weekend about returning to school. Monday morning I made him oatmeal the way he liked it—almond milk, brown sugar—and held my breath as I took the ipecac out of the spice drawer. Squeezed a few drops into the cereal and mixed it in. Kept my hand on the bowl a few moments before I picked it up, wondering if I should go through with it. I was still holding my breath, though I hadn't realized. I let it out, then brought the bowl to the table and set it down in front of him.

It's hard to describe what it felt like to do this, knowing it would make him so sick. It's for his own good, I told myself over and over. *Short-term pain for long-term gain.* When he was nearly two years old and loved his pacifier too much—it was affecting how his adult teeth would come in later—the pediatrician advised me to cut it in half while Will was napping. "That way he won't associate it with you, he'll think it happened while he was asleep. You don't have to be the bad guy." So I did this, though it kind of killed me. Took a scissors and snipped straight through the thing he loved, the thing he could count on to comfort him. I heard him stir when he awoke, and went in to the crib to get him. He was holding up the destroyed pacifier, asking me to fix it. "Oh, it's broken," I said, in a tone of sorrow I hoped would convey to him that it was beyond what could be repaired.

"Broken?" He knew the word, but obviously he

had never in his short experience of the world considered that it might apply to his binky. Too young to know enough to ask how or why, or to understand how easily a binky could be replaced. That was the first time I ever saw in his face the shock induced by the most savage of life's jolts.

He ate the oatmeal quickly—you know him, he never leaves enough time to eat. Very often he forgets to thank me for the breakfasts I make him, but not that morning; he got up and rinsed the bowl, then kissed me—kissed me! Did he think that kissing his mother would grant him some magical resistance to the thing so hell-bent on crippling him?—before grabbing up his backpack and heading out. It was too late.

I'd done some reading about how to treat emetophobia, and they said exposure therapy—like the way they bomb-proof ponies not to startle at sudden noises—could be very effective. You expose yourself to the thing you're afraid of, and find out it isn't so bad. Eventually, you stop being afraid of it.

I wanted so much for him to stop being afraid. Look at the lengths I went to.

Well, I guess I don't need to go into too much detail about what happened, after he left the house. Ipecac takes effect in about half an hour, and it was as he was walking into his homeroom that it kicked in—triggered a severe, uncontrollable spasm in his stomach muscles—and he did what he'd been afraid of doing for so long, puked his guts out in public. And not in front of strangers, but among the kids he'd gone to school with for years, including some friends, yes, but also those who thought he was a freak (his word, not mine) because he did tai chi instead of soccer, because he always had to sit at the edge of the classroom, because he was friends with Derek Foote. And (he was convinced) because he didn't know who his father was.

He vomited up his breakfast and much, much more on the threshold between his homeroom and the hallway, meaning that they were all trapped in the classroom until the janitor came to clean up. There was some delay—the janitor's day hadn't officially started yet, it took some time for him to be tracked down—so Will could not escape everyone's reactions, as they could not escape the sight and smell of the mess he had made. "Hey, you want fries with that?" somebody yelled, amid the cries of disgust. A girl in the back said, "Oh, my God, I'm gonna puke, too," and retched a little over the wastebasket. The teacher tried to settle everyone down, but there wasn't much she could do. Will slumped to the floor and hunched into himself, his gut still heaving even though there was nothing more to expel.

Needless to say, my plan backfired on me, or at least I thought so at first. As soon as the janitor had finished his work, everyone rushed to the hallway and on to their first class, except for Will, who walked out of the school without telling anyone and called to ask me to pick him up. I was expecting the call; I hadn't logged into my work queue yet. Instead I paced in front of the window, praying to the big elm though I wasn't sure what for, waiting for whatever came next. The ride back home he spent bent over, his face pressed against his knees. "I'm so sorry," I told him, reaching across to place my hand on the back of his neck. Feeling it, he jumped.

"It's not your fault." He sat up in order to speak, and I saw that he was crying. I couldn't tell who this upset more, him or me. "Mom, I *have* to see somebody. I need an emergency appointment or something. Isn't there somebody you work with, who you could call? Who'd take me right away, like *now?*" I opened my mouth to respond, but before I could, he kept talking. Which was just as well, because I'm not sure what I would have said. "This is as bad as it's ever been. This time it actually *happened*. Here I was thinking it would never actually come true—that I just had to find a way not to *feel* sick, even though I knew I probably wasn't going to puke. Now I've done it, now I know it *can* happen. It could happen any time. I'm not going to be able to go anywhere, ever."

We were almost home. I looked straight ahead through the windshield instead of at him. "It *is* my fault," I murmured. "Oh, my God. Honey, I made a terrible mistake."

"What are you talking about? How was that your fault?" He jabbed a finger behind us, toward the scene of his mortification. What had I been thinking?

I waited until we pulled into the driveway. I turned the car off, but remained in my seat without moving to open the door, and he seemed to understand that I wanted him to do the same.

"You got sick back there," I said, knowing that things could never be the same again between us, "because of something I gave you."

"What are you talking about?" he said again.

I kept my eyes averted from his. "I want you to know that I really thought it might have the opposite effect. I honestly thought it might work."

He waited, and I knew he saw no point in repeating his question another time. I told him I had put ipecac in his oatmeal.

"What the fuck is ipecac?" He'd never said *fuck* in front of me before, and I tried not to flinch.

"It's a thing you use to get kids to throw up, if you think they might have swallowed some kind of poison. It's an emetic. A syrup. It comes from the root of a plant."

Why did I say that last thing? Did I think he might feel less chagrined, or less angry at me, to know it derived from nature?

"You've got to be kidding me." His throat was raw from the vomiting, and the words came out ragged. "You're kidding, Mom, right?" I saw that he was begging for me to confess this, though I don't why that would have been any better—to have kidded him about such a thing.

I told him I thought what I read was true. I told him I had no idea the reaction would be so severe. (This was a lie; I'd watched my mother give the syrup to my sister once, after she'd gotten into the Borax under the kitchen sink. I would never forget how sick Steph was—what her face looked like, the terrible sounds—but I remember my mother saying the ipecac had saved her.)

I told Will I'd give anything to take back what I'd

done. At this he opened the car door and got out slowly, then walked slowly into the house. He stayed in his room, with Scout as his consoler, for the rest of the day and night, saying he wasn't hungry for dinner. At one point I did hear what I thought were the sounds of him doing some tai chi movements, but I couldn't be sure. I slept hardly at all that night, because the guilt kept waking me up.

But the next morning, he sat down to breakfast and ate the eggs I served. He even tried a joke, wondering out loud whether it was safe to drink the juice I poured for him. When I tried to apologize again, he said we could just forget about it, if that was all right with me. Even though I know better—that it's impossible to "just forget" such a thing—I agreed, eagerly. We never spoke again of what I'd done.

And you know what? After that, the emetophobia didn't bother him as much. By a lot, actually. I guess maybe it's come back a little lately, that's what it sounds like, I don't have any details. Have you witnessed it in him yourself? You can imagine that it wasn't easy for him to go back to school the next day, but he did it, and when he got home and I asked how it went, he shrugged and said that a few people had called him *Spew* or *Hurl*, but then that died down and things seemed pretty much back to normal. After a few days, he wasn't feeling the nausea in class anymore. "I guess I had an inflated sense of how big a deal it would be to other people," he told me. "I guess it wasn't that big a deal."

In short—I would say to Sosi—it worked. What I did,

as terrible as it sounds. Did he mention *that* to you, too, as part of "the ipecac story"?

But you poisoned him, I hear her say back to me. If it is her voice I hear.

I was just doing the best I could by him. The same goes for what I told him about the man whose biological matter mixed with mine to make this boy Sosi and I both love. And it's true—despite how much Will might want me to, I can't bring myself to call that man a "father."

I watched to make sure Trudy had gone into her own house before I unlocked Grettie's and stepped inside. Everything was in order, as I knew it would be. Grettie has always been the kind of person who cleans up pots as she cooks, alphabetizes the books on her shelves by their titles, and uses a ruler to draw a line after the recipient's name when she writes a check. In college, I used her notes instead of my own, even if we'd been sitting next to each other in the same class. People are often surprised to learn how organized she is, maybe because her appearance suggests the opposite: even indoors, that frizzy hair flies away from her face, and she never bothers to try to keep it in place with an elastic or band. It makes her look untethered, unrestrained, free. But it also gives the impression that she doesn't care. It's a false impression, which anyone who wants to be in her circle must come quickly to understand and respect, or else be refused entrance.

Even when Cam and Bella were toddlers, you would never find a stray toy on the stairs or a piece of cracker under a sofa cushion. Those kids had been taught from before the age of walking that it was their responsibility to keep their play areas neat. I thought it was too much to ask of children, so I always helped Will tidy up after himself. It had an unfortunate effect, which was that even now he leaves plates in the sink for me to wash and laundry for me to do. Well, soon enough he'll have to learn to take care of these things himself, the hard way. Unless Sosi is willing to pick up where I left off, but that's not my problem.

In the kitchen I found a surprise: an empty tube of Pringles overturned on the counter, surrounded by crumbs. Grettie always bought Pringles because she said that if they had to keep potato chips in the house, at least they'd have ones you could stack. There was no way either Grettie or Jack would have left the house for a week-long vacation knowing that those crumbs were there, or without putting the empty tube in the recycling bin. Feeling a small but distinct uneasiness, I set the tube upright.

No sign of the trash trucks yet; no sound of them even on a street in the distance. I walked upstairs and wandered into Grettie and Jack's bedroom, feeling vaguely guilty even though I told myself they would not have minded.

It was rare for me to be in their house without any of the family present. In fact, I couldn't remember if it had ever happened before. Although I had been in her bedroom plenty of times, sitting on the bed while Grettie got ready for us to go somewhere together. With anyone else, it would have bothered me that I had to wait. But since it was Grettie, I never minded. I liked watching her dry her hair, slap on some foundation and blush, and run a lipstick across her mouth. I liked watching her pucker her lips at the mirror. I've been watching her do that for almost thirty years.

I walked over to look at the photographs decorating her bureau. There were pictures of family, of course. But where did she keep the one of the two of us from Halloween of our third year living together, dressed as Thelma and Louise? We kept the framed picture on the mantel of our apartment in Amherst, over the fireplace that didn't work but made the room feel cozy. When she moved out, I had a duplicate of the photo made, so we could each have a copy where we lived. I always kept mine on my desk—first in my apartment in Allston, now in the one I share with Will. But in her bedroom I didn't see Grettie's copy of us, in its distinctive red frame, anywhere.

Without quite thinking about it, I opened her top bureau drawer. Underwear, bras, balled socks. No photograph. I straightened one of the bras before shutting the drawer.

I knew she kept her journal in her nightstand. Of course, I would never read it without her permission. I slid the nightstand drawer open, just to make sure it was where she still kept it. Yes. But instead of the leather-bound journals I remembered, she was writing now in a spiral notebook, which was open face-up to the last page she'd filled in a few days earlier. I took it out.

Afraid to go on this trip. J. says I'm catastrophizing. Trying to believe he's right. On the next line, undated so that I took it as an afterthought, she'd written *Really can't wait to get away.*

I admit it, seeing that felt like something of a punch. *From me?* I thought. She really couldn't wait to get away from *me?* There was no evidence of this, but instinctively

I felt I understood what she meant.

Telling myself I was in the process of returning the notebook to where it belonged, I flipped back through the pages to an entry she'd made in March: *Bert not doing well.* This time the hurt—though I know it sounds silly—came from the fact that she wrote my name out instead of using the more intimate initial, as she had with Jack. *She's completely undone about spring break. I can't blame her, but on the other hand, it's her fault for not letting Will know what's happening. Almost called him myself to tell him, but J. reminded me this is between them.*

It had never occurred to me that Grettie might think about contacting Will, without telling me. I suppose it's not that big a stretch—she is his godmother, after all—but as far as I know, aside from the birthday cards she sends him, they don't communicate except when the three of us are together. I wouldn't have expected her to have his number, or for him to have hers. I was glad she decided against telling him how upset I was at not seeing him during his spring break, on top of not having seen him at Christmas. That was for me to let him know, if I wanted to.

Although to be honest I'd been a little relieved, on top of the sadness, when he sent me a message to say he'd be staying on campus during the break to work for his advisor, that second week in March. They could get so much done when other people weren't around, he wrote. When there were no classes for his advisor to teach. I'd been trying for months to figure out how to tell him that the cancer had come back, and that I'd begun treatment for it, before he actually saw me (which I guess would have let him know instantly), but I hadn't come up with anything. This way, I had more time.

It was wrong to read Grettie's diary, I knew that. I put it back in her nightstand, under the piece of her childhood blankie she still rubbed between her fingers at night before falling asleep. Was Jack aware that she did this? Once, I had been the only person who knew. Of course her husband also knew it, I told myself. And much, much more than I ever would. That's what being a partner meant.

It was hot in the house, hotter than outside, because naturally they'd closed all the windows before they left. I considered opening one, but I was afraid I'd forget to shut it. Instead I went into the bathroom and dabbed cold water on my face with my fingers, not wanting to use a washcloth or a towel because Grettie might notice. I dried my fingers on the bottom of my blouse, then checked the mirror to see how I looked, though I made sure not to lean in too close. I could have looked better, but I've also looked worse. Too late, I realized I'd wiped off the minimal makeup I put on before I left my own house in anticipation of seeing the therapist. Well, too bad. It didn't matter how I would look to him, did it? I tried to convince myself of this.

When I was halfway down the stairs, I heard movement in the kitchen. Somebody else was in the house, which was supposed to be empty. It wouldn't be Cam or Bella—they were out of town, at work and camp. I froze—what to do? Sneak back up the stairs and try to hide, until whoever it was left? But what if, instead of leaving, that somebody had heard my movement, and decided to come upstairs to find its source?

I decided to stay where I was and continue hoping that whoever it was would leave by the back door. Once I heard it shut, I would look to see if anything was missing, and call the police.

But instead of that happening, Trudy Foote's drop-out son Derek walked into the family room. He headed to pick up the remote to the TV, then lowered himself onto the couch. Not flopped back, the way Will would have, but set himself down carefully onto the seat cushion, with a measure of respect he might have shown for furniture he'd been invited to occupy as a guest.

As he leaned back he caught sight of me there on the stairs, yelped, and jumped up again. He looked as shocked to see me as I felt to see him. "Oh, my God," he said. "Mrs. Chase. What are you doing here?"

Will's friends always called me *Mrs.*—it was what they had been taught. I laughed, the radical and foolish laughter of the immensely relieved. Instead of some stranger who might have killed me, it was only a boy I knew. I guess he wasn't really a boy, the same way Will isn't, but it's hard not to think of them both that way. "Derek. Doesn't it make more sense for me to ask you?"

It appeared to mean so much to him, the simple act of my using his name, that I had to look away.

He set the remote down and stood up. If it had been anyone else it would have made me nervous—who am I kidding, I probably would have run out of the house screaming for help—but because it was Will's old friend I only noted how much taller Derek still was, of the two of them. "I'm not hurting anybody," he said. "I'm not taking anything. Well, except some chips." He pointed toward the Pringles can on the kitchen counter. He smiled a little, as if he thought I might join him in pretending he'd made a joke. When I didn't smile back, he said, "Okay, fine. I'm leaving, I promise. I just needed to hide out for a while, I just needed to get away." He didn't have to say from whom—I knew he meant his mother. "And I didn't break in, I know where they leave their spare key."

How did he know that? I asked. He told me he'd been the one to feed their now long-dead cat William Butler, years ago, whenever the family went away on vacation or holidays. When he said it, I remembered offering to perform this task once when Jack's father died and they all had to leave abruptly for Galway, but Grettie told me the Foote boy would do it, he was reliable and she thought he liked the chance to get out of his own house and spend some time in hers.

I walked down the stairs toward him so that we were on the same level. When he took a step back as I approached, I felt for sure I was in no danger. I told him that I'd come to replace the trash and recycling bins in the backyard, but since they hadn't been emptied yet, I'd decided to wait to see if the trucks would come anytime soon.

"They could have asked me to do that." Derek's tone was one of injury. Then it seemed to dawn on him why Grettie and Jack might not have enlisted his help. "But I guess they wouldn't, since they hate my parents so much."

"I wouldn't say they *hate* them." Grettie wouldn't have used that word. It was disdain, not hatred, that she felt for the people trying to block Arcadia Glen.

"Don't tell my mother, but I don't agree with her about that." Derek gestured out the kitchen window, and I moved closer to see the backhoe poised to begin digging the foundation of a new house. Probably to signal that he had every intention of winning his fight to relocate the old graves, the developer had let the machine sit there, mid-job, through the winter and spring. "Didn't you ever see *Poltergeist*? You start digging up dead people, you got a problem on your hands."

He was trying to distract me, I realized. Again he wanted me to laugh or at least smile, something that would let him know I wasn't about to call the police. I watched him shift from one foot to the other, at the same time pushing brown curls away from his eyes. His mother had said more than once, in my presence and also Derek's, that his hair was wasted on a boy, he should have been a girl with all those curls.

I looked down and saw that he'd taken his shoes off—the pair of Skechers was lined up neatly by the back door. He was in his sock feet, and the socks looked clean. They looked like the kind of socks Cam wore. Had he taken them from Cam's drawer? Perhaps sensing my suspicions, Derek kept talking. "My mother's a total poser with these protests, in case you couldn't tell. She doesn't give a shit about history. And she goes on and on about nature, but she's never spent a day in nature in her life. She doesn't even like to sit on our screened porch." At this I did laugh, and he looked up surprised.

"Then why's she doing it?" I asked.

"She just wants to get her name out there, I think. It makes her look like she stands for something. Like she's not wasting her life."

Well, I could understand this. "Did she actually say so, or are you just guessing?" Not that I didn't believe it about Trudy, I was just curious about how frank she might have been with her son.

But he didn't answer my question. When I saw that he'd cast a worried glance at the crumbs on the counter between us, I understood suddenly—much later than I should have, later than I would have if it hadn't been so hot out, if my brain had been working entirely right. "It's you, isn't it? You're the one breaking into people's houses."

Derek flushed. "Of course not. Of course it's not me."

I just looked at him. Was he waiting for me to apologize for my accusation? Instead I said, "You're the Snack Burglar."

This time instead of cringing, he punched a fist into his palm. "So you're laughing at me, too."

"I'm not laughing, Derek." This time, hearing me say his name, he looked wary rather than touched. "Why would I laugh at a thing like that?"

Instead of answering he cupped a hand under the counter's edge, swept the crumbs into it, then opened the hand over the sink before running the water hard. "I guess you're probably going to tell the police what you think," he said. "About me being the one."

I hesitated. He'd made us all nervous, invading homes this way. It was a crime. I knew that by rights, he should be punished.

But to be honest, I didn't really care if some family in this snooty town lost a sleeve of crackers to this poor boy who'd had things so tough his whole life, having the screwball parents he did. And he'd been Will's friend all those years.

Knowing it was probably wrong of me, but feeling unable right then to figure it all out, I said okay, I wouldn't tell anyone. "But you have to promise not to come into this house again, ever. Or any other houses—I mean it, Derek. I'm going to come back here later today to take care of those bins, and I'm not going to tell you whether it's five minutes or five hours from now. If I find you here, I won't just call your mother—I *will* call the police."

He thanked me, and I saw his shoulders trembling.

"Why are you doing it, anyway?" I asked.

You would have thought I'd asked him to explain photosynthesis or something—that's how blank he looked. "I don't know. I guess I just like to see all the family rooms. Eat something that isn't on my 'safe' list. Something that isn't good for me. I don't even think I have food allergies, I think my mother just gets off on having a kid with 'issues.' Even though I haven't been a kid for a long time, I'm eighteen fucking years old. Oh, sorry." He had to pause for breath; all of that had taken a lot out of him. "You must think I'm insane, right?"

"Nobody thinks you're insane, Derek."

"My mother does." He said it without emotion. "She thinks I need 'behavior redirection'. She's trying to get me into some program that said they'd have a bed open today. I don't want a bed in a program, I don't need a bed in a program, but nobody seems to care about that."

He was getting himself all worked up, which was bad for both of us. In an effort to calm him down I said, "You just said it yourself, you're eighteen. You don't have to go. And if you did decide to go, you don't have to stay."

He snorted. "That's easy for you to say. You don't understand how hard it is to just leave, sometimes, even if they haven't pink-slipped you. I know you don't know what I'm talking about, but trust me, it's true."

Oh, I knew what he was talking about! But I couldn't say so. And how could I have forgotten about the pink slips?

"What kind of program?" I asked.

He shrugged. "You tell *me*. Some place where you meditate, where you do a *half-smile*. Whatever that means. I read their brochure." He gave me what might have been an approximation of a half-smile, or maybe it was actually a sneer at the idea of it.

I was tempted to tell him, though of course I would not, that I knew a lot more than he guessed. The half-smile had been described to me as a "distress tolerance skill"; in the middle of a stressful situation, you lift the muscles in your cheeks just slightly—just a little Buddha smile, the therapist said—and somehow this movement is supposed to make you feel better. Somehow, it tricks your brain. According to research, the therapist said, it causes you to perceive that you are in a better mental state than before the half-smile, and this perception, in turn, actually triggers a better feeling. Maybe not by a lot, the therapist conceded. But maybe just enough, when *just enough* makes all the difference.

The therapist wanted me to try it in front of him. Now, that sounds creepy, but at the time I thought he just wanted to make sure I got the maximum benefit out of the exercise. We'll do it together, he said, but I was too self-conscious. I told him I'd do it when I was by myself, and that night I half-smiled into the bathroom mirror. Then again the next morning. I was surprised to find that it worked, kind of. But of course, I forgot about it the next time I felt really agitated, and the time after that. Then the half-smile left my mind completely until I was reminded by the intruder in Grettie's house.

"She's probably doing the best she can," I told Derek, meaning his mother. "But I'm sure you know that. And I'm sure it doesn't help."

"You got that right." His shoulders relaxed, which made me feel better for him. "Hey, how's that genius son of yours, anyway? I saw him at a party in Allston last week, but he didn't see me." I assume to remain in my good graces, he wiped the counter with the towel Grettie kept on the oven door, then replaced it in a neat fold. "He probably wouldn't even remember who I am."

"Of course he'd remember." Why would Derek say such a thing? They'd been friends, they'd had sleepovers. "But whoever you saw, it couldn't have been him." I didn't intend to let him stay much longer; already I was feeling complicit in the way he'd invaded Grettie's living space, I felt disloyal to her. "He's not in Boston—he didn't come home for the summer. His advisor needed him to do research. So he got an apartment near school, he's living up there with his girlfriend." Though I had complicated feelings about Sosi myself, it made me glad to be able to tell people that Will had a girlfriend.

Derek snorted. He must not have realized he was going to, because he apologized right after. I said, "What was that supposed to mean?"

"Nothing. Sorry. You're probably right, it was just somebody who looked like him."

"Of course I'm right," I said.

"I mean we never really saw each other all that much, once I stopped taking tennis."

"Remember that awful pro?" I didn't mention that I'd run into the guy on my way to the hospital that morning; the shame of possibly having been flipped off by him was still with me, though of course I wouldn't have mentioned this to Derek. "The one who ran you so hard one time you puked?"

He made a small, jerky motion with his head. "That wasn't me who puked."

"What?" But even as I asked, I understood what he was telling me. Who it actually was that the pro had called a pussy. Like so many things lately, it was both a shock and not. "Well, never mind," I said quickly. "You slept over at our house sometimes, you remember that, don't you?"

"Of course I do. That was awesome. Those pancakes you made in the morning, and you let us watch cartoons."

Once, Trudy Foote called and asked if Derek could sleep over at our house on a Friday night because she and Fenton needed a night out, they were having so much trouble with Derek that they didn't know what to do. I wondered why she didn't just hire a babysitter, but I couldn't ask without having it sound as if I didn't want her son to come over. Derek arrived with his own pillow—non-allergenic, he explained to me—and a laminated index card he handed to me with a little reluctance, a little chagrin. On one side was a list of *Derek Foote's Safe Foods* and on the other a list of *Derek Foote's Forbidden Behaviors*: "biting, scratching, kicking, spitting, deliberate burping, bathroom noises (other than involuntary), cartwheels in house."

Reading it, I had burst out laughing, and Derek looked alarmed. "Oh, honey," I said, "It's okay. You can do cartwheels in our house if you want." I tried to make him feel better by telling him the card was cool, it was like he had a driver's license or something. A year or so later he probably would have used the word "lame" about my saying such a thing, but since he was only six he beamed at me, which made me love him.

"Did you know," Derek told me now in Grettie's kitchen, "that I always wished *you* could be my mother, instead of her?" He nodded toward his own house next door.

I was at a loss about how to respond. My first reaction was pleasure; then it occurred to me that he was probably setting me up to go easy on him. But I thanked him anyway, and said that was nice to hear.

This seemed to relax him further. I watched eagerness—or was it abandon?—inflate his face. "You know, sometimes I think about doing something big, something bad, like—I don't know, burn down those houses or something." He pointed out the window at the first, interrupted phase of Arcadia Glen.

It took me a moment to catch up to his words. "What? Did you just really say that?"

My reaction appeared to take him aback, as if he couldn't understand why such a remark would alarm me. But he didn't retract it. Instead he nodded, slowly, and I almost got the feeling that he was enjoying this, the idea that he might be freaking me out.

"You're not serious," I said, hoping he'd take it as a declaration of fact rather than a question. "Why would you say such a thing?"

He shrugged—well, it was more like a jerk of the shoulders he might not have been able to control. "I just want to get it over with. Prove her right, finally, about what a fuck-up I am. She wants me to have issues, I'll show her issues!" He was trying to make it sound hilarious, but the words came out with a desperate edge. "How perfect would *that* be, if she got her way about keeping the affordable people out, I mean saving the planet, because her son burned the houses down?"

All of this came fast and it was hard for me to follow, but the danger was loud and clear. "I don't believe you mean that," I told him, trying to keep my own voice calm.

"But if you do, maybe you *are* insane."

It wasn't what I'd intended to say—it just came out. But instead of looking insulted, he smiled, and I felt a chill. "You'd be burning your own house down with it," I went on, I *babbled* . . . what was I doing? Trying to reason with him, as if that made any sense. "This house. The whole neighborhood. It's been so hot lately, you don't know how far a fire like that would spread."

Now he laughed outright. "Wow, I really had you going there for a minute! You actually think I would do a thing like that? It should hurt my feelings, but I won't hold it against you. I heard what's happening. I know you're not—yourself."

What did he mean by that? Whatever it was, I didn't like it. How dare he say such a thing to me? "Of course I think you would do it," I told him. "It's the next logical step from the things you've already done. Like calling in that bomb threat at graduation. If you didn't want to go, you didn't have to. But a lot of us were looking forward to it. Why would you do a thing like that?"

He squinted, so much that his eyes virtually disappeared. I'd forgotten that about him, the narrowness of his eyes. "I didn't, Mrs. Chase," he said. "I know everybody thinks I did, but that wasn't me, either." He said it quietly, as if he wished he could avoid causing me the pain of understanding.

At this I had to gasp a little and bend over the island between us. He retreated a few steps toward the back door, then paused with his hand on the knob. "Listen, I'm leaving now, okay? Would it be the worst thing you've ever done if I asked you not to tell my mother you saw me here?"

His mother! What about the police? Did he think he was going to get away with what he'd said a few minutes ago, the threat he'd just made about torching Arcadia Glen?

But I knew it was in my interest not to give away what I was thinking. I promised him I wouldn't tell Trudy.

He looked at me longer than I expected, when I knew he was eager to leave. My blood fizzed for a second or two. Then he thanked me quickly and turned the knob. But before he could escape, I called him back. "Derek," I said, "you're not going to do anything stupid, are you?" Giving him one last chance to persuade me. I was willing to let him if he tried hard enough, if only because I didn't feel up to calling the police or anyone else.

"No. Of course not. You know me, Mrs. Chase. I was just funning." Hearing the word he and Will had used as children, I braced myself against the counter again.

Before he slipped out the door, he mumbled something. "What?" I said, hearing a frantic note in my voice. I opened the door again, and from the yard he turned back and called, "Good luck, I said."

"With what?"

"I don't know. Just ... everything." He waved a little, then hopped the fence into the half-raped woods before I could wish him luck, too.

Even before Derek was out of sight, I decided that despite what I'd told him, I would not be returning to Jack and Grettie's later that day. The idea of the obligation hanging over me while I was with the therapist—knowing that I still had a chore to perform, even such a simple one—added to the considerable anxiety I already felt about the appointment. The only alternative was to load the bags of garbage and the recyclables into my trunk and drop them off at the dump, which was located on my way to the therapist's office. That way, after the appointment, I would be free. All I'd have to do was get myself home, where I could collapse if I needed to, on the chaise or in my bed. (I knew I might have to sit in the office parking lot for fifteen minutes or a half hour before starting the drive home, but that was all right; there was a time that this had been routine for me.)

Needless to say I was not thrilled about putting garbage in my trunk, but I figured it would only be in there for a short time, it shouldn't create a lasting stink. First I filled the cloth shopping bags I keep in my car with all the loose bottles and cans and cardboard (as well as the empty Pringles can) to be recycled, and returned that bin to the garage. Then, holding the bags at arm's length, I placed them in the trunk and wheeled the barrel away from the curb. Of course, because it was Jack and Grettie's garbage, the bags had been secured tightly and neatly at the top. This gave me some measure of assurance as I closed the trunk, started the car (it took only three tries this time, it was getting better), and headed toward the dump, or what is more properly called, in this town, the municipal waste facility.

Hauling away other people's garbage! Virginia Woolf would be able to turn that into a metaphor that meant something, but I knew I could not.

To my surprise, because it was two o'clock on a Wednesday, what seemed like an off time to me, there was a line to unload at the various receptacles—glass, paper, cardboard, aluminum cans. By the time it was my turn, the trash had been in the trunk for close to twenty minutes, and I was more worried than ever about being late for my appointment.

It is at moments like these that I think most often of calling Grettie. That I *do* call her, when I can. But she was somewhere in the air now, no doubt. In flight to the surprise anniversary destination Jack was taking her to, wherever it was.

Reciting in my mind what I thought she would tell me—*You will only hurt yourself by panicking, you will only help yourself by remaining calm*—I overturned the recyclables from my shopping bags into their appropriate Dumpsters. Pleasantly surprised by my own speed and efficiency, I tried to do the same with the garbage bags, grabbing two at a time in each hand with the thought of dumping them all at once, but the one closest to me broke open as I went to upend it, spilling the contents on the ground and—I realized too late to prevent it—on me. Egg yolks and avocado peels down the side of my blouse, coffee grounds on my shoe. Grettie cooked mostly with egg whites, because Jack didn't like the yolks; they ate avocados every day for the healthy fat; coffee was one thing she splurged on, because she said there was such a big difference between an okay cup of coffee and a really good one, and choosing really good over okay could set the tone for the rest of your day. This had been true as far back as when we were roommates— we got to drink flavored gourmet coffee every morning from the subscription service her parents bought for her birthday, at Grettie's request.

The intention defines the experience, she liked to say, back then and for all the years I had known her. It was something she'd read or heard once that stuck with her. Later, Will told me similar things, passed on by his tai chi teacher. I'd never found it particularly helpful, because I rarely saw a connection between what I intended or wished for an experience and what the experience turned out to be.

For example. I now had coffee grounds on my shoe, and a strong smell floating up of dark-roasted, expensive bitterness. I tried to kick the grounds off, but they'd leaked into the shoelace holes. Trying not to panic, but panicking, I grabbed tissues from my purse and did my best to rub the yolk-and-avocado-peel mix from my blouse, but I succeeded only in making it worse, fastening the stain to the fabric.

I looked around as if someone might be available to help me—see my predicament, and offer advice or a hand—but they were waiting their turn to pull their cars in, and only wanted me out of the way. Someone shouted, "Hey! Clean up your shit!" meaning the garbage that had spilled on the ground, but even if I could have figured out how to do so, with all the interfering thoughts and feelings in my head, I was late, I was late (this was really the only thought, the only feeling), and I got back in my car and sped off without looking back to see if anyone chased me, and without buckling up.

The sudden sound of sirens made me gasp. Had they been lying in wait for me? That was ridiculous, I told myself. Nobody was trying to catch me, I hadn't done anything wrong. But it wasn't until I looked in my rearview, and didn't see any lights flashing, that I realized the piercing police wails were more distant, they were coming from somewhere else.

Those sirens had nothing to do with Derek, I told myself. He'd promised me he wouldn't do anything stupid, and besides, there hadn't been enough time.

Now the smell was not only in the trunk, but inside the car with me. The smell was me. I lowered every window all the way down, and felt relieved that it seemed slightly better as I drove toward the road that would lead me to the therapist's office. But when I reclosed the windows to test it, there it was again. I pulled into a parking lot, got out, and took a few steps away from the car. I'm sure I don't need to say that the smell followed.

I'd been sweating more than usual, I noticed, since my cancer came back. Was that a symptom of something? Besides, duh, cancer?

All these months later I still have trouble saying or even thinking it: *My cancer came back*. It was the lymphovascular invasion that probably did it. The presence of LVI in my pathology meant that some of the cancer had already traveled to my blood by the time I had surgery. Here I'd been using those two captured convicts as a metaphor, when it turns out there was a third one nobody ever knew about, who got away! Metaphorically, at least. To treat it, I went through a short term of radiation a month or so after the surgery, which the doctors said reduced the chance of recurrence from about ten to one percent. But it couldn't eliminate it completely.

The day after the second presidential debate, a month before the election, I saw blood in the toilet again. I tried to convince myself it was just the result of stress—all the news was giving me headaches, I kept telling myself not to watch and then watching anyway. But I knew enough to go and get checked out. A week later I went in to have it confirmed: the chances had been slim, but they had always been there. The cancer had recurred, in my vaginal vault. *(Vault!* The place you put things to keep them safe. I would never see that word in the same way again.) "I'm very sorry," Dr. Venn said. She did look sorry. It was all I could do not to say to her *It's okay.* "I'm just so sorry that you have to be one of the rare ones this happens to."

They could do straight chemotherapy, she said, but my situation was such that she recommended we "think outside the box." I couldn't help a small smile and wondered if she found that as unfortunate a pun as I did, but I didn't ask. She went on to describe something called sandwich therapy: chemo followed by radiation followed by chemo again. "I won't lie to you," she said, "it'll be rough. But there's promising research that suggests this may be the route we should consider for you now."

It was up to me, she continued—she knew it was a big decision, there was my quality of life to consider. But if I were her sister, she would encourage me to go ahead. I appreciated that, her making it personal. It was probably the reason I decided to take her advice.

But I told her I'd have to put it off until after Christmas. Actually, until the second week of January, when my son would go back to school. I didn't want to be in the middle of treatments when he came home for the holiday, I didn't want him to see me that way, potentially so sick. I could start as soon as he went back, then be done with the worst of it—and back in recovery mode—by the time of his spring break.

I could tell by the doctor's reaction that she didn't like this idea. "I wouldn't recommend delaying," she said, but when I told her it was the only way I'd go through with it, she sighed and said okay, it was my decision, she would write the order for me to begin on January sixteenth.

She was right about the treatment being rough—that's putting it mildly! But I don't see any reason to spend any time describing what I went through. Remembering it is bad enough. People always say about a bad experience that they wouldn't wish it on their worst enemy, but I don't mind saying that I would. The chemo-radiation-chemo sandwich—yes, I think that would be just about the perfect punishment.

The schedulers said I might want to have someone accompany me to each treatment, but it was also possible for me to take a cab or hire a car to and from the hospital. I deliberated about mentioning it to Grettie. I wanted her to be there, but I knew how much it was to ask. Instead of asking, I told her what Dr. Venn had said I needed, how often the treatments were. I could tell that Grettie wanted to say she'd bring me in every day I had to be there, but we both knew this was too much of a commitment: she had her classes, she had her family, she had her life, and she couldn't put hers on hold just because mine would be. I remember thinking that if I had a partner, it would be different; a partner's life is on hold along with yours. But she was not my partner. She is not my partner. How many times have I had to remind myself of that, in the past twenty-five years?

In the end I scheduled most of my rides with a home health service that provided transportation. But Grettie brought me when she could, which turned out to be at least once a week for the five-week regimen, and sometimes twice. She made sure to be there for my first chemo appointment, and for my last. During the drive in for the first, we listened on the radio to plans for the inauguration; Grettie switched it off. During the drive in for the last, we left the radio on to hear about the latest court blocking the president's travel ban. On a weekend in between, when I didn't feel well enough to accompany Grettie and some of our friends into Boston for the Women's March, she used her phone to have them send me a video of all of them chanting and cheering, and on her way home she stopped by to bring me soup and the sign she'd carried during the rally: *Love Never Fails*, which she propped up at the end of my bed so I could see it when I opened my eyes each morning and before I closed them each night. It's still there, though I'm going to have to move it; the other night I woke up and mistook it for a person standing there, it scared me to death.

During these weeks, I came to realize that I would never feel ecstatic again. A rise of the heart that hits no ceiling, that speeding rush of joy. Even in the printed word—*ecstatic*—I've always seen the features of faces crinkled in rapture, felt the stirrings of it in my own gut.

So what if I'm done with all that? I tried to tell myself. Ecstasy is for children, who don't know any better. For young people who still have their lives in front of them. For people who don't really get that they're going to die.

After the first treatment, Grettie took me for ice cream. After the last, she brought me home to collapse on the couch, where she sat next to me and tucked the shorts strands of remaining hair behind my ear. It was something I'd always done with my little sister when she sat on my lap as we watched TV after school, waiting for our mother to get home, but I'd never told Grettie about that. How did she know to make just this gesture, how did she know it would bring me comfort like nothing else would?

"Why are we friends?" I asked, not quite having realized I was going to.

She paused in her hair-tucking, looking startled. "What?"

"I mean, it's obvious why I like being around you. Why everyone does. But what do you get out of it—our friendship?"

"Oh, Roberta." She put a hand on her chest. "Do you really not know?"

I had to look away. "So you're going to miss me?" Okay, this was why I'd asked the first question—I saw that then.

"Oh, Bert." I felt a twinge of guilt at the distress I saw in her face. "Of course I'd miss you, if it came to that. But please let's not talk this way."

After my last treatment, she held the pail for me to puke in. Fed me ice chips, put a cloth on my head, brought me clear broth and then the pail again. We watched TV together that night, more episodes of the British crime drama she was so fond of. I confessed that I hadn't gotten into it that much, I could barely understand what the characters were saying. "Oh, you should have told me," she said, "I can fix that," and she turned on the subtitles, but it was too late; I'd already missed too much of the story. She went into my bedroom and came back with the comforter, then wrapped it around both of us on the couch. I wanted to lean against her but when I hesitated, afraid she would pull away, she said, "Oh, Bert. We're beyond all that now, aren't we?" and reached to pull my head gently against her chest.

She did know! At last, the answer to Sosi's question, which (to be honest) had been my question, too. Had Grettie known all along, or had it dawned on her after we both moved here and later began raising our children together? I couldn't tell whether it made me sad or happy, that she'd known for years how I really felt, and never ventured to bring it up.

But it didn't matter. All that mattered was what it felt like to lie against her, matching the rhythm of my breath to hers in the blue glow of the TV. I wanted to stay awake to savor the feeling, but it was too much for me. As she watched the show with a captivation I envied, I fell asleep—finally it happened!—in her arms. How wrong I'd been, I thought as I dropped off, to think I would not feel ecstatic ever again.

And after all that—after I delayed my treatments because I wanted to have the holiday at home with Will—he blew me off. Well, that's a harsh way of putting it. But that's what it felt like. When I texted him to say that I knew he didn't want me to contact him but I wasn't sure when his vacation started, when to expect him home, I didn't hear from him and didn't hear from him and then he called—he called! I was so happy to hear his voice, before I realized he was delivering bad news—to say that he was sorry, but he'd decided to go with Sosi to her family's over the break.

"What do you mean?" I asked, feeling stupid. "You won't be here for Christmas?" We'd never missed one together; the prospect of not seeing him on Christmas was something I hadn't considered. He promised he'd come home for spring break, which—*really, Mom, when you think about it*—wasn't so far away.

I should have just told him on the phone that day, that the cancer had come back. I could have written a note, I could have typed an email, I could have sent him a text. I could have called him on Skype or FaceTime. But I didn't want to do any of those things—I wanted to be there with him when he heard it. In person, face to face, without any screens or electronic signals. I wanted it to be part of home for him, not school.

But he has not come home. So I have not told him.

After we hung up, I knew I should call Dr. Venn's office to see if was in fact possible to switch back to an earlier set of dates for my treatment regimen. But my nerve failed me. What if this was my last Christmas? Did I want to spend it puking into a bucket, and missing my son to boot?

I have a hard time answering some questions, but this wasn't one of them.

My sister called on Christmas morning. We reminisced—if you could call it that. *Reminisce*, to me, conjures an image of happy people sitting around together, talking about happy things. This was on the phone and it wasn't happy, but maybe it still counts.

"I woke up this morning thinking of all that phlegm," she said, when I answered.

"Merry Christmas to you, too." Then we both laughed a little, even though what we were talking about was our mother's death.

"Sorry. It's just that it was so vivid—I dreamed there were rivers and rivers of it. I was about to drown." In the background I heard her take a sip of something—coffee, I hoped. It was eleven o'clock where I was, which meant it was eight a.m. out there for her. But it was a holiday. "If she'd gone in sooner, do you think they could have caught it in time?" Whenever I spoke with Steph she was obsessed to some degree with the question of whether our mother might have lived longer if this or if that, to the point that I never bothered to answer anymore.

And this was my opening, I realized. Speaking of diagnoses, of catching things in time. But I let it pass. With it being Christmas and everything, I didn't have the heart (not just for her sake, but mine, too) to tell her the latest news about my health. Besides, if those were ice cubes I heard rattling, now that I focused harder on the sound, who knew if she'd even remember, once we got off the phone?

"Oh, well. Never mind," she sighed, the way she did so often. I've been listening to that sigh all my life—first from our mother, then from her. "What are you guys doing today? Going to Grettie's, I assume?"

Steph lives in California with her husband, a cyber-security specialist named Harley Davidson, I kid you not. He's not a biker himself, but both of his parents were. If you were to meet him, he would tell you very early on that he started going by *Hal* in kindergarten, inspired by the name of the computer in *2001: A Space Odyssey*. He likes to brag that he can hack into any system, given enough time. He's quick to add that he doesn't do anything illegal, but I have my doubts. How else would he have taught my son the things he'd needed to know, to go as deep as he did in my hospital database?

Steph and Hal don't have any children. I remember

asking her about it, during a visit she made to see us shortly after Will's second birthday. She and Hal weren't married yet, but they were planning on it. We sat outside as Will played beside us in the courtyard. This was back when he used to say *Look what I can do!* all the time, before somersaulting or twisting his arms into a pretzel or hopping on one leg.

"Are you guys going to start trying right away, or wait awhile?" I asked her. It was lunchtime and I served iced tea, but she asked if we could open the Chardonnay she'd seen in the fridge, that I was saving for dinner.

"I don't think we're going to have them at all," she said.

This surprised me. When we'd met her at the airport and Will ran straight into her outstretched arms, I saw a look on her face I thought I hadn't seen there before, or at least not since she was little: the kind of happiness that makes you close your eyes so you can shut everything else out, and savor how good you feel. Yes, she'd looked ecstatic.

He has so many women who love him! Yet how many of them would he trade to know just one man—that one specific man?

"But why?" I said. "You'd be such a great mother."

"I don't think so." She lifted her glass to drain what was left, but it was already gone. "I can't drink *and* have a kid—I won't do that to her."

I've always wondered whether Steph realized that she said *her*, as if she possessed knowledge of a destined daughter about whom she was making decisions before the child could be conceived. "You don't understand, Bert. I get Mom, now. This"— she gestured at her empty glass—"is the only way I can be, in the world. I've found something that works."

"What are you talking about?" Sure, she'd had her wild times in college. But I'd never seen her out of control. "What do you mean 'something that works'?"

She looked pained, as if it hurt her to have to have this conversation. Or maybe it hurt her that I had to ask, that I didn't already know something this important about my own sister. "I can't explain it, and to be honest, I'm glad you don't understand. For your own sake. For his." She nodded over at Will, who lay on his back in the grass with one chubby leg folded over the other, looking up at the sky.

"It's the only way I can relax," she told me. "I mean completely. Otherwise I'm on edge all the time, even when I'm home, even when nobody's expecting anything from me. It's in my body, this perpetual tenseness. I probably inherited it from Mom."

I wanted to say *bullshit*, but I knew this wouldn't do any good. "There are other ways," I said instead. "Therapy! I went to a therapist, you know that." Though I'd never told her about the night in the cemetery, the wanting to die. I felt an obligation, as the older sister, to protect her from my own frailty, especially since I'd been at least as much of a mother to her as our actual mother had been. "Meditation. Yoga. Exercise, for God's sake."

She waved a hand as if to say *Been there, done that, they don't work. Or They don't work well enough.* Then, to signal that she'd had enough of being interrogated for the time being, she changed the subject. "It still amazes me that you had a baby. On your own like that. Like *this*. I mean, you're only thirty. What's the rush? Why didn't you wait to see if you met someone you wanted to marry, so you could have kids together, and not have to do it all on your own?"

There were a lot of questions in there. I understood that some had been spoken, and some had not. "Haven't you met any nice guys?" she persisted. "I mean, it's a big city. There must be some nice guys around."

There was a man, I could have told her. There were a few men—some before Will, and one after. That one, I even thought I might marry. But when it came right down to it, I couldn't be sure there was enough love in the circle among the three of us—him for Will, or me for him—to make it worth it. To think that the odds of us being together after a few years, or even a year, were better than the odds of us not. I didn't want to inflict a divorce upon Will, so I called it off. Soon after that, he began to have problems anyway. But I'm sure they would have been worse if the man had still been around.

On top of which—who am I kidding?—he was not *her*. I murmured something to Steph about being so busy now, as the mother of a toddler, that the last thing I thought about was going on dates.

But this didn't satisfy her. "It would be one thing if you had a boyfriend and you found yourself pregnant, and decided to go ahead and have the kid instead of an abortion." Her wine glass was empty. When I didn't make a move to go inside to get the bottle, she drew her hand reluctantly from the stem. "But to go ahead and pursue it—find a sperm bank, buy the sperm, get insem-inated ... how many times did it take, anyway? I don't think you ever told me."

"Just the one," I said, then coughed before adding, "I got lucky."

"I just don't get it. You never wanted a kid that much, at least not that you ever told me." I heard hurt in her voice. "So how does it work, anyway? How'd you decide what sperm to order?"

Dammit, I thought. Why hadn't I just decided to tell everyone, if and when they asked, that I'd gotten preg-nant having sex with someone I never saw again? Yes, it would have been completely out of character. But it was also pretty much true. As it was, once I lied about having a donor, I had to keep compounding it by coming up with answers to questions like the ones my sister was asking.

"The donors fill out questionnaires. In longhand, so you even get a sense of their handwriting." I'd done my research. "Everything from favorite color to taste in music to where they'd like most to travel in the world. The administrator picked out the closest matches to the things I said I was looking for, and sent them to me. I got about six or seven. I chose one, ordered a vial, made an appointment, and—*voilá!*" I waved at Will, who'd called to us *Look what I can do!* and was now walking in a circle on his tiptoes.

Watching him, Steph smiled; she might challenge me on the advisability of single motherhood, but I knew she loved being an aunt. "You only ordered one vial?"

"Well, they're not cheap. I figured I could always get more if it didn't work the first time."

"But what if you want to give him a sibling? I would think you'd have ordered extra, for when that time might come. In case they run out, or whatever. In case the guy—his sperm—isn't available anymore."

"Wow," I said, after a moment. "You're a Chatty Cathy about this, aren't you?"

"Sorry." She looked as if I'd hurt her feelings. "I didn't mean to be, I'm just curious."

I could see that she wanted to ask more, so I told her it was okay. "Probably no on the siblings," I said. "In fact, definitely not. But Cam's only a little older, and we spend a lot of time with him and Grettie, so it's like having a brother around. Or a cousin."

She nodded. "And what kinds of things were you looking for? In a donor. If you don't mind my asking."

"Oh, I don't know." I thought about the things I loved most in Will. "Intelligence. Sensitivity."

"Well, you got those for sure." She smiled as he came over to hand her a dandelion covered in white fluff, and told her to make a wish.

She closed her eyes and thought for a moment before blowing the wisps into the yard.

When he'd run off again, she said in a low voice, "I wished for him to have a father someday. I hope that doesn't offend you."

"No," I said, although it did, a little; the implication seemed to be that I wasn't enough. "But Will isn't going to be able to track down his donor."

"*A* father, I wished for. It doesn't have to be the biological one."

I stood and picked up my own plate, but she hadn't eaten all of her lunch. "Are you going to finish that?" I asked.

"No. Can you bring the bottle out? I assume you got a full medical history and the guy's healthy. No mental disorders or anything, right?

I could have commented on the irony of her bringing this up right after invoking our alcoholic mother and requesting a refill of the wine she was drinking with lunch. But I didn't. Instead I made my habitual murmuring sound and stacked our plates. I could tell she'd expected more in the way of an answer, but she didn't press. She remained seated at the table, watching Will, and I brought the dishes inside, put them in the sink, then did my best to regain my composure before I went back out to join them. I set the Chardonnay in front of her but declined to pour it; if she wanted to destroy herself, she'd have to do it on her own, I wouldn't help.

From across the table I watched her fill her glass, seeing on her face an expression I would have called reverent, if someone had asked me just then. "Could I see his questionnaire?" she asked, after the first few sips.

I looked at my fingernails. "No. I got rid of it."

"What?" She practically gasped. "You did not."

"Yes, I did."

"But why?"

I shrugged, trying to give the impression that it didn't

matter. "What would have been the point?"

"You did not do that," she said again. "I know you, Bert. You hang onto everything. You kept my report cards from middle school, you still have Mom's bracelet from the hospital."

"Well. Yes, I keep the things that mean something to me." It was hot under the sun that day, and all this talking was making me sweat; I ran my fingers across my forehead and they came away damp. "But the questionnaire was just—I don't know, it was like a brochure or something. Once I put in my order, once I got what I wanted, I didn't need it anymore."

She made a noise I couldn't read, and shook her head. "What?" I said.

"Didn't it ever occur to you that *he* might want to see it?" She nodded toward Will.

"I remember everything. I can tell him what it said."

"That's not the same as seeing what the guy put down. How he described himself. What his handwriting looked like, for God's sake."

I was not accustomed to having my little sister call me out on things, and I didn't like how it felt. But I didn't want to say this, I didn't want to fight. I decided not to respond, and this must have caused her to reconsider at least the tone she'd taken. "I'm sorry, Bert. I don't mean to criticize. I'm just surprised, that's all; it's not like you, to throw away something like that. I'm sure it was a hard process, the whole thing."

You have no idea! I wanted to shout, but of course I would not. It was so tempting, but I'd made a promise to myself.

"And I'm sorry I wasn't here for it. I'm sorry you had to go through it alone."

I wasn't alone, I reminded her—I'd had Grettie.

At this I saw Steph hesitate. "Did you show *her* the questionnaire?"

I shook my head. This made her feel better, I could see.

Steph and I don't see or call each other too often, anymore. It's hard for her to drink the way she wants to, around me, and hard for me to watch her do it. But we always talk on Christmas, because it was our mother's favorite time of year. She especially loved composing her annual Christmas letter. I can still conjure up the image of her sitting at the kitchen table, scribbling on a yellow pad, a glass of wine nearby for inspiration. Who am I kidding—it was a bottle, not a glass. "Both girls continue to enjoy and excel at their various pursuits. This year Stephanie took up riding, while Roberta mastered the art of the self-portrait in pen and ink."

I had "mastered" the art of the self-portrait—oh, Mom! I was a doodler. And it was not horses my sister rode, it was the back of Trent Green's Kawasaki. The year my father left to move to Texas with the wife of one of his poker buddies, my mother wrote that he was "traveling the country in pursuit of new opportunities." But that, of course, is what the Christmas letter is for. A way to imply (and in my mother's case, I'm sure, to believe) that things are different from what they are. That they are better. It always made me nervous. I knew that anyone who received my mother's letter would see right through it.

She used to leave up the red-ribboned pine wreath on our front door until well into the spring, sometimes even till summer. It still makes me nervous to see Christmas wreaths up that late in the year. Don't people realize? It makes me anxious to think they aren't paying the right attention, things aren't getting taken care of the way they need to be.

Fittingly—or was it the opposite of fitting?—our mother died on Christmas Day. The nurses' station at the hospital was draped in green and red tinsel. This was St. Elizabeth's. Christmas carols were piped in over the PA. Steph and I spent a lot of time, at the end, inventing our own version of a Christmas letter, in an effort to assure our mother that her life had been better than it was. What would have been the point of insisting on the truth, at that point? The woman was dying. And we loved her.

Will heard Steph and me recalling this during one of her visits to us when he was about ten. "I can't believe you guys did that," he said. "So the last thing Grandma ever heard was you lying to her."

"It wasn't lying," Steph told him. "Or, it was, technically, but it was for a greater good."

Will made a scornful noise. "I would never do that to *you*," he said, but it didn't really register back then, it wasn't something I imagined him someday having to decide.

I don't believe Steph and I ever regretted the things we said to our mother in the hospital. What was it she said, at the end? "Certain parts I could have done without, but on the whole, I liked it." As if life had been a book somebody asked her to review.

Since then, Christmas has always been a hard time for both my sister and me. That's one of the reasons I was surprised when Will didn't come home this year–he's aware that it's a sad anniversary. When he was growing up I did my best to hide my sadness from him, but I knew he could see it. From the time he was little he always tried to cheer me up, making a big deal out of how much he loved the presents Santa had brought.

During our Christmas phone call this year, I told Steph when she asked that yes, I'd be going over to Grettie's later.

"Just you? By yourself?"

I had two choices, the only ones any of us ever has: lie or tell the truth. I didn't like deceiving my sister, but neither did I want to hear myself say out loud that I wouldn't be spending Christmas with my son. So instead of answering her question I told her that Will had a girlfriend, whom I'd met at Thanksgiving, a nice girl with red hair who seemed to like him a lot.

This time I definitely heard ice cubes dropping into a drink. "I love you, Bert," my sister said, and then, as she always does even though I've asked her not to, she disconnected before I could say it back.

It wouldn't have mattered so much, Will not being home, if I could have gone to Grettie and Jack's house as I usually did. But this year they'd flown over to visit Jack's brother in Galway. They'd had a fight about it, Grettie said, when she called to tell me that we were going to have to change our plans. I felt bad hearing about their fight, but worse when I realized that the end of the story was that I would be alone. It was a family thing, she explained to me. Well, I understand like everyone else does that *family* is code for *more important*. Jack's brother was going through a divorce, he needed his family to be with him and his children for this first holiday without their mother.

I *understand,* I told her. *Of course I do.* But of course I *didn't!* Jack's brother and his kids have many more Christmases ahead of them; this one would probably be my last. But Grettie knew that. She knew, too, that it was the anniversary of my mother's death. But she assumed that Will would be coming home, that he and I would spend the day together.

After my sister hung up on me, I watched two episodes of Grettie's British crime drama. It wasn't quite my cup of tea, but she loved it, so I decided to stick with it. I'd just started a third episode after heating up some soup when Will called from Sosi's house to wish me a Merry Christmas. I asked if he'd gotten the box of homemade cookies I'd sent to school during final exams. He said yes, but they'd put the cookies out for everyone, because he and Sosi were taking a month off from sugar and they didn't want them to get stale.

"You're taking a month off from sugar at Christmastime?" I said, trying not to let on that I felt hurt.

A pause on the other end. "I've been having a little trouble with my stomach," he said—or at least I think he said, his voice sounded a little faint. "I was hoping going off sugar might help."

Of course I would have asked him what kind of trouble, but before I could, he said it was almost time for "the family dinner." That gave me a punch to the gut, I don't mind saying. He was the second person to hang up on me that day. I stood at the window and looked out at the big tree. *I am just a biological organism,* I told myself, but it didn't work any better for me than it had for him, back when I was so fixed on curing his emetophobia. Why had I thought it might work?

The soup was cold by the time I got back to it, but I ate it anyway. It didn't make any difference.

When Grettie returned from the trip and called to ask how our Christmas had been with just the two of us, I told her Will had spent the holiday with Sosi's family, and that he would be going straight back to school from there. I could tell from her silence that she was shocked.

Did she also feel bad for abandoning me? Of course she hadn't abandoned me, but that's what it felt like, as silly as it is to admit. "Oh, for God's sake, Bert," she said, and I didn't know whether she was referring to my having spent the holiday alone, my son's absence, or the news—still relatively fresh for both of us—that my cancer had returned. Probably all of it. "I'll be right over," she said, and then *that* was a good day.

Standing in the parking lot I'd pulled into on the way to the therapist's, dismayed to find that the smell of garbage was getting worse instead of better, I stabbed at my phone: almost two-thirty. Was it possible for me to dash home, change clothes, and still make it to my appointment on time? Well, there was no choice—I had to try.

I've spent most of my life trying to avoid feeling the way I felt as I sped toward my house. And though of course I didn't have the time for it, at the last minute before I would have passed the garden stand offering *Fay's Fresh Flowers!* I pulled over, kicked my door open, and huffed up to the mixed bouquets, where I grabbed one and slapped down a twenty. Without waiting for change, I huffed back to the car and tossed the flowers on the seat beside me, hoping the scent would attach itself to me and in even the smallest way mask the terrible smell.

I screeched into my driveway, made it inside as fast as I could, peeled off my blouse, and grabbed the first thing I could find, a tee-shirt that said *I'm a Nurse, What's Your Superpower?* (I guess this was false advertising, but it was a freebie from the hospital.) Not at all elegant, and not the way I'd wanted to look when I saw the therapist, but I didn't have time to search for something else.

Scout looked nervous, lifting his head to watch me from his bed in the living room. "It's okay, boy," I told him. "It's okay, I'll be back soon."

Outside again, pitching myself at the car, I found

Pascal standing in my way. "What's wrong?" she asked. "Can I do anything?" She must have heard my car pull up fast, and watched me bolt into my house. Fleetingly, it occurred to me to wonder whether she'd heard about my recurrence. Hard to imagine she'd known about it and hadn't approached me, but, then, maybe she figured I wouldn't have wanted her to.

"No!" I hadn't exactly meant to shout, but that's how it came out.

"If you need to get somewhere, I could drive you." She almost looked as if she might grab the keys out of my hand, but I shouted "No" again and pushed by her to get into the car. Backing out, I tried to wave to let her know I appreciated her offer, but the wheel got away from me and I had to yank at it with both hands to steer myself onto the road.

Our encounter had lasted no longer than a minute, but I could see that she still felt hurt. I never told her that it was Will's idea, not mine, to exclude her in the invitation to his graduation last year. It's a sacrifice I decided to make, to let her think *I* didn't want her there, to save her the pain of knowing it was actually him. In the end it didn't matter because the commencement didn't happen, but at the time it felt like a big deal.

I'm pretty sure it wasn't personal, this decision on his part. It was just that with his birthday coming up— the birthday he'd been looking forward to because he thought he would finally find out who his father was—he didn't need three mothers coming to watch him graduate. Maybe he didn't even want *one*.

That's how he used to put it, that he had "three mothers and zero fathers." There was me, of course. Then Grettie, whom we call his godmother even though it's nothing religious or official. She and Jack would have become his guardians if I'd died before he turned eighteen—or maybe it's twenty-one if he's in college, it might still apply. I keep forgetting to look that up.

Pascal moved into the condo across from us when Will was in preschool. She was single, too, though with no children, and we hit it off immediately, becoming friends in that way you do when it seems a foregone conclusion. The way Grettie and I had, those first days after I moved in. "Pascal," I said, when she introduced herself, "Are you French?"

No, she said. And added that if she'd known how many times she would be asked that, she would have chosen a different name.

Chosen? My ears perked up. I was intrigued by the idea of someone choosing a new name—what was wrong with the old one?

She shrugged. "I don't know, it was boring. *Patty*. I never liked it, my mother named me after Patty Duke. Every Patty I ever knew, there wasn't much to them."

Though no other Pattys sprang to mind, I gave my murmuring sound so she'd think I knew what she meant.

Going from Patty to Pascal seemed like a bold move to me—or did it not seem quite bold enough? I couldn't tell, I didn't know my own mind. But if you're going to go to the trouble of changing your name you should like what you end up with, and she seemed to like having become Pascal.

I told her she was the tallest woman I'd ever met. She shrugged again. "I get that a lot, too. Also 'the most mannish.'"

"Well, that's not very nice."

"I know. I can't help it. I'm going to grow my hair out, though. Coming here's a fresh start for me, a new leaf. I'm going to join one of those online dating sites. Have you ever tried that?"

I said No, I hadn't, but then, I was busy with my son.

Pascal told me she loved kids, and she began spending a lot of time with Will, taking him out for ice cream or to the playground or the Lego store, each week a new adventure. I told her I didn't want her to spend too much money, but she could probably tell that I was secretly glad she was able to buy him things I couldn't afford myself—Transformers, Nintendo games. Her job as a freelance auditor was more lucrative than mine and more flexible, too, because even though I worked from home, I still had to be logged in at the computer eight hours a day. She asked if we could arrange a regular day each week for her to pick him up from school and keep him at her house through a pizza dinner, so we settled on Tuesdays. I tried not to be jealous when, after a few weeks, Will told me that Tuesday was his favorite day. He always came home with some new art project she'd helped him with, a pinecone wreath or a fort made of Popsicle sticks. The few times I went on dates, Pascal babysat for him. He could go back and forth between our houses without a grownup holding his hand. We were a little family. It was wonderful, for a while. For a few years there, I stopped missing Grettie so much.

But when he was in third grade, Pascal and I had a falling-out, and as uncomfortable as it is to admit, we've never quite recovered the friendship we had before. It was over such a small thing (I saw in retrospect) that I hesitate to mention it, but why not, I'm admitting everything now. I mean, if not now, when?

Will had a habit back then of telling stories. Well, lies, if you want to call them that. At first I didn't realize, because they were so innocuous—he'd tell me the dessert for lunch in the cafeteria had been butterscotch pudding, when really it was apple crisp; he'd tell me there'd been a substitute teacher at school that day, when there hadn't been; he'd tell me they'd done a ropes course in gym, when he and the other kids had only played dodgeball.

At first I thought it was just a phase he'd grow out of, like everything else. I also thought it was something he just did with me.

But it didn't stop, and I found out that it happened with everyone, including Pascal and people at school. I discovered this only when I went to pick him up one day and another mother said how exciting it was that I was pregnant, and asked when I was due.

I had a conference with his teacher, because she said Will's lies—she used that word—were becoming bolder, more obvious. He told other kids he'd gone to Egypt over winter vacation (they'd been studying the pyramids and the Sphinx); beyond that, he told them he'd been allowed to sit in the cockpit with the pilot on the plane that took us there.

He told them his father was the president of a chocolate factory. (You can guess what book I had been reading to him at night.)

I knew why he'd told people I was going to have another baby. He'd begged me for a little brother, though he said a sister would be "not bad," too. I remember how excited I was when my own sister was born, and how much I loved having a little person to take care of. I suppose that's why it felt familiar and not foreign when I held Will close to me, after they cleaned him up and took his measurements and laid him on my chest in those first moments I was actually a mother.

Some studies show that kids who lie are highly intelligent and creative, the teacher conceded when we had our talk.

I interrupted her to say that yes, Will was both those things. As an example I told her that the other day he'd said to me, "Mom, I just figured out that life isn't a movie, because it never comes to the end."

It never comes to the end! How it hurts, thinking of that now. There's only so much remembering a person can take.

But—the teacher continued—she worried that the lying was affecting Will's abilities to "integrate socially," to "relate effectively to his peers." She asked me to have a talk with him about it. Maybe together, he and I could turn the lies into a book—I could write down the stories he told, and he could draw illustrations. This was a possible "strategy" for turning around a "negative behavior" that none of us wanted to see "become a liability."

I can quote her verbatim because I was making notes at the time, it's the kind of mother I was. Am.

I'll talk to him, I promised the teacher.

But I didn't get to it before the next time he had an afternoon with Pascal. When she brought him home that night, I could see that she felt stricken. "Roberta," she said (she'd never been comfortable addressing me as Bert, though I invited her to), "what happened?"

"What do you mean?" Beside her, Will looked confused. No, not confused, I realized after a moment—he looked guilty. "I don't know what you're talking about."

He said he wanted to check on Scout and left us to go to his room, where the dog slept at the foot of the big-boy bed. He closed the door behind them, which he hardly ever did.

"He told me you were going to die," Pascal said in an urgent whisper.

I admit that it took a few moments for her words to sink in. Then I said, "Well, we're all going to die. I'm sure that's what he meant. We had to have that conversation about Scout."

"That's not what he meant. He didn't mean *some-day*. He said you'd gone to the doctor and they'd told you you had a lump, and it was going to kill you."

Oh. That was dumb of me, I'd told him when he asked why he didn't have a grandma that she'd had a lump, and that it had killed her.

"I don't have a lump," I told Pascal, and I explained

about the stories.

Was it denying cancer that made it come for me, all those years later? I know that's ridiculous, but it's the way my mind works, sometimes.

The next night when I tucked Will into bed, I asked him why he'd told Pascal I was going to die. "Because then I'd get to meet my father! I'd have to live with him!" he said, flipping over to turn his back to me. I knew I should touch his shoulder and have a conversation, but instead I turned the light out and shut the door behind me.

I told Pascal that I thought the "stories" weren't that big a deal. She said, "Roberta, you can't just let something like this go. With kids, it's better to nip these things in the bud."

I knew I wasn't supposed to ask her how she could say a thing like that, since she didn't have any children herself. I knew how painful a fact this was to her—not to be married, and not to have a child.

She'd told me when she moved in that she'd chosen this town, a family town, hoping that by doing so, she would attract the family she wanted. A kind of "If you build it, they will come" attitude, only I could tell that it was less an actual attitude than a craving, a desire it hurt her to speak about. It made me think of what the therapist had told me once, quoting William James. As with the half-smile, if you act *as if* you feel the way you want to feel, chances are you will start feeling that way.

"But wouldn't I just be fooling myself?" I'd asked him, even though I knew I risked sounding stupid. I worried about that a lot, with the therapist. "Wouldn't that make everything a delusion?" He told me No, not a delusion—it was more of a strategy to get my mind to believe something that might not be true yet but that *could* be true, especially the more I believed it.

It didn't make sense to me at the time, though I pretended to understand what he was saying. But since then, I've come to see the value in acting *as if*. I probably do it more than I do anything else now, if you want to know the truth.

Pascal told me that what she felt about not having a child was grief. It was her confessing this, as much as the discussion about Will's habit of telling stories, that was really the undoing of our friendship, although I'm not sure she realizes it to this day. She let me know how much she wanted, and how much she needed me. That was your mistake, I had the impulse to tell her. You shouldn't show that to people, it only makes things worse. They hate you for being vulnerable. *I* kind of hated her for it, though of course I didn't say so. And it didn't last, though afterward there was always a smudge between us, a gray mark, a thumbprint she'd put there that couldn't be rubbed out.

So I knew that Will was a kind of surrogate for something Pascal always thought she would have and desperately wanted. I knew, during our phone conversation, that there was no good to come of doing anything other than thanking her for the suggestion to nip things in the bud, and telling her I would take it into account when I talked to Will about his storytelling habit.

But even though I knew all these things, I said it anyway. "No offense, Pascal, but you're not his mother."

There was a silence on the other end of the phone before she said, "I know that, Roberta. I know that very well." Her tone was one of hurt; I would have preferred it to be angry. Angry would have been easier.

I was sorry for my words even as I was saying them. Over my desk I keep a quote from Emerson: "Finish each day and be done with it. You have done what you could. Some blunders and absurdities have crept in; forget them as soon as you can. Tomorrow is a new day." Sometimes, the quote helps me forgive myself for things like the dig I had just taken at my friend—the blunders and absurdities I regret but can't take back. Other times, like this one, it helps not at all. What I'd said to Pascal was not a blunder, it was not an absurdity. It was just plain cruel, and no pretty quote from a poet or anyone else was going to make me feel better about it, which was only right.

We didn't mention the argument again. At some point, of course, the weekly visits stopped, because Will didn't need to be picked up from school anymore and because he began taking tai chi. The three of us got together for dinner every so often, at our house or hers. She still gave him presents every Christmas and birthday, and despite not being invited to graduation, she left a card with a check for two hundred dollars in our mailbox. In return, he left a thank-you note in her box without my reminding him to do so—I brought him up right. Since then, though, and especially since he left for college, Pascal and I haven't had much contact.

In the end, each of us got hurt by the other. Neither of us felt we'd been wrong, or felt inclined to apologize. I know it's ridiculous that we've let it go on this long, without finding some way to make up, but that's just the way it is. I can't forgive her challenging my behavior as a mother, and I guess she can't forgive my reminding her that she'd failed to do, or have, the things I knew she wanted most.

No, that wasn't really what came between us, the lie Will told and my resentment about her telling me how I should handle it. What came between us was the move she made one night as she was leaving, after a few hours of confessional conversation over a bottle of wine (three glasses for her, one for me). I said good-bye at the door and waited to close it behind her, but instead of letting me do this she turned and leaned, aimed her face toward mine, and pressed her lips as close as she could manage to my mouth, before I gave an exclamation and pulled away.

"What are you doing?" I wiped away the remnant of her touch with the back of my hand. "What the hell was that?"

Her expression was a mix of chagrin and injury. "I'm sorry. I thought we were both feeling it, I thought you might have wanted me to."

"No! I did not! Oh, my God." I slammed the door between us, then yanked it open again. "What would have given you that idea?"

"I don't know. It was just a feeling. I'm sorry—really, I am." She put a hand on my doorway to keep herself upright. "I didn't think it would upset you so much. I thought we were in the same boat—both of us trying to pass."

Pass. It was the word I'd used for myself when I first moved to this town, knowing that I didn't really belong in it. But Pascal meant something else. I was going to make her say it. "Trying to pass for what?"

I could tell she knew she'd already said more than she should have. I could see she regretted it. "I'll go home and sleep it off," she said, with a clumsy, embarrassed smile, and I told her that was a good idea.

That was when the afternoons with Will ended. Not right after he told her the lie about the lump I didn't have.

But it didn't bear thinking about now, as I blew through the stop sign at the end of my street and gunned the accelerator toward the therapist's office on the other side of town. What were the chances I'd get stopped? Not many police officers out and about at this time of day, and besides, I'd heard those sirens earlier—wherever that was, that's where the police would be, at the emergency.

I pulled into the therapist's parking lot with only a few minutes to spare. I stepped out of the car sniffing at myself, dismayed to find that changing my shirt had only barely subdued the smell. I dove back in behind the driver's seat, suddenly realizing that he might have been looking, at that moment, out the window. I calculated my options: Call and cancel. Call and reschedule. Don't call and don't show up. Go in and keep the appointment.

But there was really only one choice, I knew: I had to do this, and it had to be today. It was time. Taking a deep breath, I stepped out of the car again, feeling the afternoon's bewildering heat seep into my scalp. *The intention defines the experience,* I heard in my head, spoken in Grettie's voice. Well, then. Just because it had never worked for me before didn't mean it wouldn't work now. I intended to get what I needed, for myself and my son.

It was not the fancy and famous psychiatric hospital in the town next to mine that the police brought me to when they found me trying to commit suicide under the bush in the cemetery more than twenty years ago. Who am I kidding—I don't think I actually intended to let myself fall asleep in that snow.

But it's hard to be sure. Maybe I really only did it to get Grettie's attention, even though afterward I decided not to tell her about any of it. I know how pathetic that sounds, but it's the truth. She had an infant to take care of, and I hardly ever got to see her anymore. When I did see her, she was of course tending to Cam. She was tired, wrung out. She who always seemed to be able to do everything that was asked of her had finally met her match, and it threw me for a loop, seeing her like that. But not until I gave birth myself did I understand how hard it all is on both your mind and your body, having a baby to take care of. I've been ashamed ever since, that I faked such an attempt and then, to make it worse, didn't admit the truth to anyone. Allowed the therapist and the other people at the hospital to believe I was that depressed, that desperate. It's a little confusing to me even now, because I did feel those things. I can't be sure I didn't mean to kill myself, but I do remember thinking as I arranged myself in the snow under the bush that I would get up and go home before I fell asleep. But then the cops came and it was all over—I got pink-slipped into the hospital.

I always thought pink-slipped meant being fired, but I learned another meaning that night. They can also issue one if they think you're a danger to yourself or someone else. The slip they showed me was actually pink. With that pretty piece of paper they can throw you in the nuthouse for a minimum of seventy-two hours, after which you can plead your case to be released.

My commitment was not to the fancy and famous hospital in the next town, but the ugly blond-brick building two towns away in the other direction. I'd been there only once before, for a mammogram, but that was in the basement—the psych unit was on the top floor. Bars on the windows, of course. I hardly slept at all that first night because they put me on short checks, which meant that the door opened and a flashlight was shined on me every fifteen minutes.

In the morning I saw the therapist assigned to my case, the same one I had made the appointment with for today. He approved my release after the seventy-two hours, on the condition that I continue to see him as an outpatient at his regular office, the one I drove to now after moving too quickly at the municipal waste facility and spilling garbage all over myself.

The waiting room occupied the same physical space it had back then, but I barely recognized it. In fact I did a double-take and checked the number on the door, wondering if I'd entered the wrong suite. But no, it was the right room—it only *felt* new, felt different. There was actual art on the walls now, small abstracts and a figure or two. If I remembered correctly, the walls themselves had been off-white and held a few cheaply framed, standard-fare posters—buds, ponds—that seemed to aim at being ignored instead of noticed.

He must be doing better financially, now, than when he'd had the assignment of Doctor on Call at the ugly hospital. The walls of the suite were painted orange, which might sound garish but actually looked nice. Prints in similarly bright colors hung above the sofa and behind the chair I chose to sit in, this time, because I always took the sofa back then.

Back then the only reading material on the coffee table was *Reader's Digest* and a copy of that day's newspaper, often stained by coffee or smudged by fingerprints. Now there was an assortment of magazines, ones I would actually like to read: *The New Yorker, Vanity Fair.* If I were a patient now, I thought, I might come early to look at the magazines, and to prepare myself for my appointment. I used to avoid getting to his office before ten of the hour, so I wouldn't have to see the patient before me walking out. Today, I didn't care. But it didn't matter anyway, because given how much the garbage and recycling chore set me back, not to mention the frantic trip home to change my clothes, I arrived at the waiting room only a minute or two before my scheduled time.

The sound of the office door opening was the same as all those years ago. Despite the fact that I no longer cared, it ignited the little bit of tinder remaining in my chest, which I hadn't known was there. The spark led me to realize (with no small measure of dismay) that it was possible I did still care, at least a little.

He'd always had a little routine when greeting me: two steps from the inner sanctum, facing forward. Then a forty-five-degree turn to where I sat. Now I saw that the routine had not changed since I'd seen him last, all those years ago. "Celia Santoro?" he said, with a pleasant, solicitous air. In an instant, his voice pulled loose the careful knot I'd secured inside myself.

Though I had used the false name in booking the appointment, it never crossed my mind that he might not recognize me. When I was younger—at the time I knew him—I fancied myself beautiful. He'd told me this, and so had Grettie. A few men I'd dated said the same.

But now I knew that I looked like a forty-seven-year-old woman—one who'd been treated for cancer, to boot. My hair had grown back in, but it was too short. And I'd lost more weight, with the recurrence, than the first time around.

But beautiful or not, sick or not, shouldn't he remember me?

I'd prepared myself for that moment—the meeting of our eyes, his sudden understanding of who I was. To be honest, I hoped to flummox him. I'd never seen him flummoxed. That was a word I've always loved, and a state I looked forward to seeing the therapist in.

It didn't happen, at least not at first. He addressed me by the false name and showed me in. I saw him wrinkle his nose—ever so small a movement, almost imperceptible. It's me! I wanted to cry out. The urge to confess it to him felt overwhelming. *It's me who smells like garbage!*

But I'd made a promise to myself about how this meeting would go. No matter how much I wanted to, I would not allow him to see that I was vulnerable. I took the chair across from him, lowering myself into it slowly. Though my stomach muscles had long since recovered from the surgery, I was still in the habit of moving with more care than I had before my original diagnosis.

"I'm glad you finally made it in," he told me. "I remember you had an appointment arranged for last fall, but then you canceled."

I'd almost forgotten I'd done that, booked a time with him after Will and Sosi left in such a huff over Thanksgiving weekend. I was afraid Will would do what he in fact did end up doing—refuse to come home until I gave him what I wanted, which I couldn't do without talking to the therapist first. The appointment was for December thirteenth, and when I recognized the date as the anniversary of the one all those years ago, I canceled. I'll do it later, I thought. I had enough to deal with: more blood in the toilet, the news that the cancer had returned, scheduling treatments. I got distracted, I wasn't up to facing the therapist. Not that I was up to it today, either, but ... I had no choice but to be here, my options were running out.

I made my murmuring noise and nodded, as if to indicate to him that I was glad I'd made it in today, too.

Across from us, against the wall, was the couch. *The couch*. Surely it could not be the same couch. But I could not be sure ... how was it possible that I remembered so vividly so much of my time in this office, but not the couch? The style, the upholstery? The smell? It could not be the same couch, I decided.

Even as we faced each other straight on, he failed (or pretended to fail; how would I know which?) to realize who I was. Clueless, Will would say.

He'd gotten older too, of course. His hair was thinner, and mostly gray. He himself was thinner and smaller. Back then he'd worn more casual clothing—Oxfords, corduroys. I had never seen him in a tie. But obviously, he had come up in the world. He wore a tie today, and a sport coat hung on the back of his desk chair.

There was a time when I would have wished I could shrink myself enough to fit in a pocket of that coat. I believed he could protect me from anything that might hurt me, including myself.

But he was just another person, I saw now, who was going to die like the rest of us. Observing this in someone I'd had such strong feelings for, once, might have made me feel pity now. But not for him. Though I knew better than to believe I could overpower him and strangle him with his tie, I thought about it.

"Maybe you can tell me a little about yourself, to get started." A pad of paper and a pen sat on the table next to him, but he didn't pick them up. "Tell me what you hope I can do for you."

Though I couldn't be sure, it felt as if part of my brain lit up at those words, and I thought I remembered them from the very first time I'd ever seen him, in the ugly hospital. Back then, I had not been able to answer; instead, I cried.

I would not cry today.

"I am not," I told him, "Celia Santoro." I wondered if he noticed I had to pause in the middle, to take a breath. "You don't know who I am," I added—a statement not a question. Just in case I was wrong, I left a space for him to correct me.

A pause on his side now. "Should I?"

After I strangled him with his tie, I would stamp my foot on his mouth and press down with all the weight I could muster. But no, I needed to keep my head. "My real name is Roberta," I told him. "Roberta Chase. I'm guessing that rings a bell?"

A quick narrowing of the eyes behind his glasses, a quick intake of breath. His temple pulsed and he shifted slightly, but enough so that I could see discomfort in the movement. Bingo, I thought.

But he conceded nothing. Instead he said, "You're sick." At first I thought he meant that it was deranged of me to have made this appointment. Then I realized he was referring to what I looked like. I folded my arms across my chest and forced myself not to answer, I didn't want him to think he could get back the upper hand.

When I didn't respond, he reached for the pen and paper. "Refresh my memory, if you would."

Refresh my memory! I would twist his arms one at a time behind his back until they snapped. "The last time I came to this office," I said, "you raped me on that couch."

It was a figure of speech—not the rape part, but calling it "that couch." Of course it could not be the same couch, nineteen years later—could it? Why could I remember not a single detail about the couch?

I had not thought I would be in a position of having to put words to what happened that day. I thought he would recognize me immediately, and try to prevent me from getting a foot in the door.

He moved not at all now, just stared at me without blinking. Without writing anything down. "That's an extraordinary claim."

Claim. Implying something possibly not true, which means possibly true. He had given himself away by not denying it, but I doubt he realized this himself.

"No, not extraordinary. Just an ordinary fact. You raped me, and I never came back, even though I had appointments scheduled. Now that I think about it, you might even have sent me a bill for the ones I missed." I snorted a little, though laughter has come to pain me. Why had I not remembered before now, about the bill?

I saw that he was studying me, and the expression in his eyes was a combustion of alarm and hatred—I read them as clearly as if his pupils spelled out the words. *Hatred.* In all my imagining of this moment, I had not expected to see that emotion there. Though of course I should have. What delusion had I allowed myself, to think that he wouldn't hate me?

"I remember now," he said. He tried but failed to hide that he needed to clear his throat. "I saw you at the hospital, in a very depressed state. A suicide attempt, something involving a cemetery. As I recall, you were struggling with your sexual identity." He sat up straighter, as if reciting these facts energized him. "Some confusion. You went out with men, but—wait a moment, I have it—you were in love with your college roommate. I forget her name, something unusual. Something from literature. She was living with someone else, set to marry him. Have I got it right?"

I sensed that he was rattled, but not yet flummoxed. Probably he thought there was some way he could talk himself out of this—to talk me out of whatever fantasy he would now try to convince me I suffered from.

"Yes," I said. It was a relief to confirm this part of his account; he *did* remember. "So you decided to help me out. You said, I'll show you how to like men. This will make you better. You told me, *This is what you need.*" I reached for the chair's arms to steady myself. "And then you raped me."

It's a terrible word, *rape*. Not many people can hear it without showing something behind their eyes. But he was one of them; I might have just said *biscuit* or *piano*, for all the reaction he showed.

It was very hard to sit through the long moments that followed. He watched me, and I could see his mind working, in a way I had not been able to all those years ago because I was so focused on myself. I wondered if he was going to break down and beg my forgiveness, or laugh and point to the door. I could have imagined either response, from what I saw in his eyes.

And, oh, something else! Something I would not have recognized, of course, when I saw him back then. He had the same dent over his eyebrow as my son—now,

I recognized the little pulse that went in and out, in and out, giving away how hard he was working to focus, or to make a calculation.

"Is that it?" he asked. "You came back just to say this preposterous thing? For what purpose? What is your point?"

I took a bigger breath than I ended up needing, and choked a little as it came out. "The point is that I got pregnant. I had a baby." Okay, he was flummoxed now! But I couldn't enjoy it. I had not anticipated that this mere word, baby, was what would threaten to make me break down—the memory of Will's skin against mine, the way he rubbed my arm as he fell asleep. I forced myself to sit up from my slump; it was a bad habit I'd always had, which the last diagnosis only made worse. "Will. He's eighteen now. I never told him about you—I never told anybody—but it's gotten more complicated, now."

I hadn't decided before I went in whether I'd tell him Will's name. It just slipped out; or was I trying to appeal to the therapist's humanity? If this was the case, it was a bad judgment call.

He made a sound I interpreted at first as another dismissal, though a moment later it occurred to me that he'd allowed a bit of his own panic to escape, like steam from a kettle. "Impossible," he told me, rising from his chair. "You need to get out of here, or I'll call Security." He went to his desk and picked up the phone, but did not dial. The only other time he'd ever gone to his desk, back when I was seeing him, was the day it was raining so hard out, thunderstorming really, and he had to get up to take from his drawer an inhaler, which he used discreetly, his back turned to me, looking out the window.

"No, not impossible." I remained seated. His agitation was giving me courage. I've always been that way; whenever I am nervous about something, but see that someone else is *more* nervous, my own nervousness vanishes. "You had me pinned," I said. "You were between me and the door. I wanted to get out, I couldn't get out, that's rape."

He stared at me long and hard; I could feel his eyes on me, even though I didn't look back. Quietly he said, "I remember now. This was always part of your presentation; you worried that you sometimes encouraged others to think of you as being something you were not. Something about your mother. And Christmas letters ... do I have that right? This must be one of those times."

I growled at him. I growled! If we hadn't been talking about what we were talking about, I would have been amused by the sound I made. He took a step back, and I thought he might topple–I wanted him to.

"I could identify those two moles on the inside of your left thigh," I told him. "You said, 'That's my extra pair of eyes, so I can see you better down there.'" At this he drew in more breath than he should have needed, and I realized he recognized his own line. "I could compel your DNA. There's no statute of limitations; I looked it up."

These were not things I had planned to say, but I didn't want him to know that. I did my best to keep my chin steady, and to avoid letting the room swim in front of me.

It was his turn, but instead of speaking, he made an

impatient waving gesture with the hand not holding the phone. *How dare you*, I thought, feeling sour phlegm rise in my throat. "We may have had consensual intercourse, I'll grant you that. I shouldn't have agreed to it, but I thought you were saner than you were." *Agreed* to it! "Saner than you are." He jabbed a finger toward me as if I might not understand who he was speaking to, otherwise. "Look, doctors have affairs with their patients all the time. Maybe not all the time, but often enough. They don't have to lose their careers over it, there are ways of working it out. So whatever you think you have over me—this *rape* threat—it would be your word against mine."

I was tempted to be scared by this. But that was what he wanted, I realized.

Then a familiar dismay overtook me. Was it possible that I was wrong about the rape part? He sounded so certain. And he was so angry at me ... was the way he looked the way somebody might look if he'd been accused of something he didn't do?

But no: I remember the smell of his breath, and the way he forced that tongue tasting of peppermint mocha into my mouth. I was wearing jeans that day, and I went home with the waistband ripped. Feeling sore on top of stunned. I fell asleep in the bathtub, woke up two hours later in cold water. My thighs and my wrists were bruised. I remember his voice in my ear grunting *This feels good, don't tell me it doesn't. Stop moving, you're pissing me off*

Also: if he hadn't done it, he had no reason to be angry—right? If he had nothing to be afraid of from what I said.

He put the phone down. I thought he might come at me, as he had that day—he looked as if he wanted to—but instead he flexed and unflexed the fingers of both hands at his sides. An exercise aimed at relieving stress? I wondered if it had worked for him, before now.

The pulse in his temple had gotten more pronounced. Thank God that was the only piece of resemblance, or I would have had a much harder time all these years. Aside from the little dent and the asthma, Will took after me.

"You've made a mistake, coming here," he said finally, when it became clear to both of us that he was not going to call Security or anyone else.

"I could have pressed charges," I told him. "I *should* have. But you were too important to me. Did you know that? It took me a long time just to realize what you'd done was rape." I'd said the word more times in five minutes than in the past twenty years. It got easier each time; I didn't know whether I should feel glad about this or not. "It doesn't matter that it was that long ago, I'm still within my rights to file a paternity complaint."

Slowly, he came back from the desk to resume his position across from mine. I wondered if he was thinking about using my purse strap to strangle *me*.

"I do want something from you," I told him. "But it doesn't involve pressing charges, or a paternity test."

As he shifted in his chair I caught a familiar look on his face, but it wasn't because I'd seen it in him before. "You feel like throwing up, don't you?" I said, as the bells in my own head went *Ding ding ding*. It was exactly the way Will looked when I asked him to clean up after

Scout or when the urge to vomit grabbed him suddenly by the throat.

"Jesus, you smell." The therapist leaned back in his chair. "What, do you live in a Dumpster?" With a hand that shook slightly, he took a sip from the mug on the table beside us. Did he still drink that peppermint mocha? Peppermint was known to settle the stomach.

"My son has emetophobia." I refused to say Will's name again—not for the therapist's sake, but my own. I wouldn't say *our son*, either. "I bet he got it from you."

"I don't have emetophobia, for Christ's sake. But why does it not surprise me that he does? With you for a mother."

"What's that supposed to mean?" It didn't mean anything. I had read all about it, there was nothing to suggest that a mother had anything to do with a child's phobia, about vomiting or anything else. But hearing him say it upset me, that should be no surprise.

"Do you remember," I asked, to take his mind off the way I smelled, "how you used to leave the newspaper out there in the waiting room? Do you know that I tore a corner off a page once because it had a thumbprint on it, and I thought it might be yours? And I took it home with me. I actually thought that if I touched the thumbprint, it would be almost like you were there with me." He looked down at the crease in his slacks—did what I said move him, somehow? "I had no idea if it was yours or not—anybody could have been reading that newspaper! It was probably some sociopath who had an appointment right before mine."

He gave a small smile, which chilled me; it was not a good smile. "I don't treat sociopaths. I never have. It doesn't do any good—they don't get better."

"Ha." Now I was the one who smiled. "So it's a matter of integrity? I guess I don't have to point out to you the irony of your saying that."

"It's not integrity. Treating them would just be a waste of my time." Grudgingly, silently, I gave him credit for being honest about this. You can see why it screwed me up so much to see him, and always had—I never knew what kind of person he really was, the one I wished him to be or the one he seemed to be, more of the time than not. The one who continued speaking now. "Look, just get on with it. What do you want?" I heard *How can I get rid of you?* but I don't think he said it out loud.

Get on with it, I echoed to myself. "My son wants to know who—fathered him. All his life I've told him it was an anonymous donor, that he'll never be able to find out, that it's just something he needs to accept. Make peace with. I thought it was working, he hadn't said anything about it for a long time. But when he turned eighteen last year, he asked me again. And when I wouldn't tell him, he got angry and cut me off—I haven't seen him since Thanksgiving."

It took my breath away, saying those last words. Maybe because it was still a shock to me that it had been that long, but it was also because I hardly ever say so much at once. And—it was a little hard, now, for me to breathe.

"I came here to ask if you would let me tell him," I said. "That it's you. I don't have to use the word *father*,

I never have. And of course I wouldn't tell him about the rape, or even that you were my therapist. I'd just say we met at the hospital or something—that wouldn't even be a lie—that we fell in love" (I had to pause and run my tongue over my lips, before I could go on), "that one thing led to another, and he was conceived."

He grimaced when I said the part about falling in love. I tried to avoid letting it sting, but I failed to slam the door on that feeling fast enough.

He let a long time go by, without speaking. Well, it might not actually have been a long time, but it felt that way. Then he said, "Why the fuck didn't you just get an abortion? I would have paid for it."

It made the room shimmer, hearing him use the obscenity from that chair. So many times I'd sat across from him and listened to his voice, which had been so kind and gentle (hadn't it?), the opposite of the cruelty I heard in it now.

I told him I'd considered an abortion, though it wasn't true. What was harder to admit to myself, when I could bear to, was that I'd gone through with the pregnancy because I wanted someone to love, and someone to love me back. It also gave me something to share with Grettie—motherhood, being a mother, we were in it together; we've ended up sharing more because of that than we ever could have, if I'd been alone.

"You've never told anyone?" the therapist asked. "Not even ... your woman friend?"

I shook my head. "And I'm not saying we have to tell anybody now, except him. I'm not asking you to tell your family." I had been feeling hot, but now I shivered; I wasn't sure if it came from my body or the room. "I'd leave that up to you. I'd tell him it was delicate, he'd have to be content with knowing who you are, maybe you two could just have dinner from time to time. He'd have no claim on you—I'd make sure he understood that."

He laughed. *He laughed!* I felt the sound curdling in my stomach. He laughed as if I'd said something truly funny. "Maybe we could 'just have dinner from time to time.'" When I heard my own words mocked by his voice, I thought I might pass out. "You're a lunatic, you know that? You have some goddam nerve."

Even though I did not have my wits entirely about me, I wondered how he could say such a thing, when I had already mentioned the possibility of criminal charges. Was he calling my bluff? "You really are sick. You don't get it, Roberta, do you?" He had never said my name before, I had never heard him say it. I told myself, *Stop shaking.* "There's nothing I could possibly want less in this world than to meet any fucked-up kid of yours."

I gasped. Then I couldn't stop gasping. I had decided before I came in that even if he didn't agree to be identified or to meet Will, I would still tell Will the truth. I would give him the sanitized story I'd just recited, about how he had come to be conceived; I would ask his forgiveness for not telling him sooner; and, for his own sake, I would advise him not to go against the therapist's wishes and try to contact him.

But the worst I'd expected was that the therapist would be shocked by what I told him. Possibly even hurt because I'd kept this news from him, all these years. In all my imagining about this encounter, I had not envisioned the anger I'd seen in him today. The vitriol, the violence. I hadn't thought of that word, *violence*, the day he raped me. To myself I said he got *carried away*. But now I saw that it had been just a corner of what I peeled off now.

"Why did you really come to see me?" he asked, in the same tone he might use to inquire what kind of cars were available for him to rent. My gasping seemed to flummox him not at all. "After all this time?"

I'd anticipated this question, and prepared an answer. I'd intended to use the phrase *revised circumstances*, the one that struck me so hard in a Joan Didion book; she was writing about her daughter who, six months after she walked down the aisle as a happy bride, fell sick with pneumonia, septic shock, and a brain bleed, all kinds of terrible things. The daughter ended up dying. She did not want to talk about those revised circumstances, Didion wrote. She wanted to believe that if she did not "dwell" on them she would wake one morning and find them corrected. I read this right after my second diagnosis (Grettie lent me the book) and, oh, I felt that way myself! I've thought about them every day since, those words. Revised circumstances. My circumstances have been revised, I was going to tell the therapist. But in the moment, I forgot.

I wasn't just sick, I told him. I was dying. He asked me what kind of cancer, and when I answered he said, "But that's very treatable. Most women don't—"

"I know. Lucky me, I drew one of the rare short sticks." What I would have given, twenty years ago, to have had something so dramatic to tell him, certain as I would have been of his sympathy and concern! But it would have been fake concern and sympathy, I saw now. It would have been aimed at getting me to come back to him, week after week. "Plus, I waited to have it checked out, longer than they told me I should."

He didn't ask why, and I understood that he couldn't have cared less; asking me *what kind of cancer* had just been to buy some time while he considered how to get rid of me, once and for all.

Instead what he asked was, "But why did you come in person? You could have sent me a letter. An email. Or called."

I was absurdly proud of myself for producing, on the spot, an answer that sounded plausible. "Those things could leave a trace. A record of some kind. I didn't want to do that, I wanted it just between us."

What I didn't say: "I wanted to see you. I thought it was possible you might be able to explain everything. Why you did what you did to me, and how sorry you are. I had this fantasy that you would be happy about the idea of meeting Will and getting to know him." *I had this fantasy*, I would never say, *that I've been wrong all these years—that you aren't that person, it didn't happen the way I remembered.* Though I didn't really want that, either, because wouldn't that be a tragedy of its own?

I left it at that: "I wanted it just between us."

I wished I had been able to say more. Why didn't I tell

him, "Hey, I have an idea, why don't you *act as if* you care about what I'm saying? *As if* you're sorry for what you did back then, *as if* you want to know your own son, *as if* you give a shit about anybody besides yourself?"

But of course, I didn't. He said, "How much," and got up to cross to his desk.

"They told me maybe six months. But that was a while ago."

He gave another brusque wave at my answer. "No, *how much* do you want?" He had removed a checkbook from the drawer.

I didn't understand, at first. Then it dawned on me, the pieces clicking into place. "You want to buy me off?"

"That's really what you came for, isn't it? If you actually think I'm a rapist, which I am not, I find it hard to believe you'd want your son to know that's where he comes from."

"But I wouldn't tell him that, I already said so." It was true. Will would never get over knowing he'd been born out of a rape. He'd take it into himself, drink it like a poison that would always leave a trace, think it meant there was something wrong with him. That he was conceived in violence, in a crime, might mean to him that he was defective, a demon, some kind of freak. That this was the source of all he perceived to be wrong with him; worst of all, that he might turn out to be such a person himself.

The therapist laughed again. "And I'm supposed to trust you?" His eyes moved to the photograph on his desk, the one of his wife and children. I knew the therapist hadn't intended for me to see him glancing at the photo, but I also knew he could tell that I had. "Look, I'm sorry about what's happening to you. I mean that." (He didn't mean it.) "But let's make this work for both of us, shall we?"

I wanted so much to believe him, to believe he was sorry. Yet I could not.

"You said he was eighteen. Is he in college?"

I nodded. I no longer wanted him to have any information about Will, but he knew he could ask whatever he wanted, and he knew I would answer. We both knew it. It was in the air between us and always had been, my compliance to his will.

"Well, he'll need money for that, right? Once you're gone. I'm guessing you don't have a whole lot saved up— not enough, anyway. And I'm assuming you don't have a spouse." I had not given him any of this information; how could he tell? But I knew the answer: I wore it, my aloneness, like a wrong-fitting shawl. "So how about if I take care of his tuition, and we call it even. You never tell him anything, and I never hear from him.

"And I mean *ever*, Roberta." There it was again, that thrill at hearing my name in his voice. It made me sick to feel that way. "If he ever tries to see me, if he ever calls or writes, I'm sure you can imagine the kinds of things I could get him to believe." He paused before delivering the final blow, and as I watched the light widen behind his eyes, it occurred to me that a part of him was enjoying this. "Including things about you, which might or might not be true."

It had been a mistake, telling him about the emetophobia. Now he knew my son was vulnerable on the inside, now he had something on him.

His tuition—what it would cost for him to go to school for the next three years—was one of the things I had planned to talk to Will about, once I told him the cancer had returned. Grettie had already told me that she and Jack could help out, but I said No, he can take out more loans, that's what they're there for. Then let us loan it to him, she said.

What the therapist was offering meant that Will could finish his degree without owing anyone. He'd have enough to manage, losing me, without also having such a debt hanging over his head. "You're trying to bribe me," I said.

"No." He sat down and wrote a check, then ripped it out of the book. The sound scraped me inside. "This is not a bribe. This is me giving in to your blackmail."

He handed it over. When I saw the amount, it was all I could do not to say *Thank you*.

Recovering, I said, "How do you know I won't still come after you?" I felt myself flush. "This check doesn't change anything. I could still file a claim and force you to submit your DNA."

"But you won't. Because what would that get you? Nothing that you want." He smiled—it was the smile of a winner.

"I wouldn't be so sure," I said, trying to sound threatening. But I don't know how to sound like a winner, and this was obvious to us both.

Why had I thought it possible that I would get a response from him any different from the one I had just received? Because I wanted it to be so—plain and simple. I wanted him to be the man I'd thought he was, before he raped me.

But of course he is a different kind of man entirely, the kind of man I never want my son to know, or to fear he might be.

He waved me off—*shooed* me is more like it—and I scrambled to open the door, slip through to the other side, then shut it behind me before he could follow, though of course he had no such intention. A patient waiting for some other therapist, under the bright abstracts, looked up from where she was thumbing through *Vanity Fair* and then shot me a look of understanding and sympathy: *Tough session, huh?* I clutched my purse tightly to my side as I huffed to the door of the suite, which was heavier than I remembered; it fell away from me and I reached for it again, but by then the other patient had gotten up from the couch and come over to open it for me. I thanked her, trying not to gasp again, and felt her watching me as I made my way down the corridor and toward the stairs.

It's the check, I thought—the check is what's making this harder, my purse is heavier than it was before, it's what's weighing me down. Of course this makes no sense now, but at the time, it did. Finally I made it out to the parking lot and my car, where I yanked the door open and collapsed behind the steering wheel, which I used then as a pillow because I had to—I couldn't help it—I had to take a little nap right there, before I could go on.

In the car I had to sit longer than I expected, to calm down and clear my mind. Well, not *clear,* exactly—no way that was going to happen, after the scene I'd just left—but to give my heart a rest from the racing it had been doing the whole time I was in the therapist's office.

More from instinct than anything else, I called Grettie. I figured she wouldn't answer—figured she was in the air over Brussels or Dubrovnik or some other equally exotic place Jack was whisking her off to for their anniversary celebration. But no, she said when she answered. As it turned out, he'd actually rented them a room in an inn on a lake in New Hampshire. Less than two hours north. "He knew I wouldn't want to be that far away from you right now. What's going on?"

Oh, Jack, thank you. I breathed the words to him in my mind, the deepest relief I could remember ever feeling. Bless his Irish heart! Whatever resentment I'd ever held toward him, or he'd held toward me over the years (and who knows if I was even right about that, I was questioning everything now), he'd set it aside because he knew she would be distracted, couldn't fully enjoy the occasion the way he hoped she would.

Did I feel guilty about this? Well, yes. But to be honest, the good feeling it gave me was more distinct, stronger, than the bad. And it was not lost on me—as it was not lost on Jack, I'm sure—that every anniversary after this

one would be his and hers alone, no chance of my interfering.

Though I wanted nothing more, I couldn't answer
her question. I couldn't tell her I'd gone to see my old
therapist, or what he had said. What he'd threatened me
with. In fact I couldn't say much of anything for the first
minute or two, just had to sit there behind the steering
wheel and catch my breath. Finally, when I could manage
a few words—"I'm scared, please help"—she told me not
to worry, and to hold on. She asked where I was and said
I should stay right there. But I couldn't, I had to move
while I had the energy, while I could still make it to the
bank.

I had sweated all the way through my tee-shirt, and for
some reason my eyesight was dim; maybe it was because
of the fluorescent lights in the therapist's waiting room,
I wasn't used to them. It was so hot that the flowers I'd
thrown onto the passenger seat were already dying, and
it took more energy than I would have guessed to open
the car door and drop them in the space I was leaving.
By the time I pulled out of the parking lot, things looked
a little brighter, but not as bright as they should have. I
slowed down for what I thought was a speed bump, but
it turned out to be just a shadow—of what, I couldn't tell.
All of that made me decide to be more cautious in my
drive to the bank. I went slower and found myself grip-
ping the wheel more tightly than usual, even though I remembered from Driver's Ed that this isn't really a good
idea, it just makes you tenser. I tried to relax, and when
I got to the bank I sat for a while in that lot, too, before

making sure I still had the check in my purse, and then getting out.

Typically I do my business using the ATM, but because of the check's weight, its enormousness, I knew this would be too risky–I had to go inside and give it to a teller. And what would he or she make of a check in that amount, drawn on a physician's business account, especially when it was submitted by a woman who tried but failed to hide her distress during the transaction, and smelled of garbage to boot? Tellers are no doubt trained not to show any reactions, I'm sure. And, of course, not to ask any questions about what a check is for. Yet they'd wonder, I knew–looking at me through the window, and maybe watching me after I left.

Well, what did I care? I did care, but I knew I shouldn't, and knowing this provided a little relief.

This was a good outcome, wasn't it? This check. Even though it wasn't the one I had asked for. I tried to persuade myself of the upside. Now Will would have enough money to finish college, even some left over for graduate school, though he was aiming at fellowships for that. Maybe the therapist did not want to acknowledge fathering my son (let alone raping me–at this point, he was right, I would not get anything out of his acknowledging that), but the check was a form of child support–right?

It was–for God's sake!–the least he could do.

Inside the bank, I was glad to see that there was no one else in the line. Two teller windows were open, a woman and a man. I chose the woman out of instinct, even though I know from experience that it didn't necessarily mean she'd be the more sympathetic. She was older than me, but not that much. Her name badge said *Stephanie Lee*. I was tempted to tell her I had a sister named Stephanie, then decided not to. What would she care?

She waited for me to state my business. I opened my mouth, but nothing came out. I reached into my purse to remove the check, and one of its corners slit my finger. Who knew a check could cut that deep? Even in the state I was in, I recognized it for the metaphor it was—the therapist's money would hurt me, hurt my son. It was already doing so, before I had even put it in my account ... "Look," I said to the teller, "I'm bleeding."

She peered through the space between us, then plucked a tissue and handed it to me. I pressed it against the wound. It seemed to me that she frowned as she observed this, though I couldn't be sure, I was concentrating too hard on a very simple task. "Would you like some water or something?" she asked quietly. "Would you like to sit down? There's a bathroom in back."

I thanked her and shook my head. I thought about saying *Why would I want water for a paper cut?*, but I didn't, because she was only trying to be nice.

I put my purse on the counter. Inside it, I saw that the check showed a little spot of blood. "Is there anything I can do for you?" Stephanie asked. Behind me, I could feel that a small line had formed, of people who wanted her to get rid of me and take care of them.

All I had to do was pull the check out, sign it, and hand it over. I knew this, but my mind would not issue the instruction, my body had an objection to the plan. "Maybe I'll come back later," I told her. Could she hear me? It seemed I was whispering. "Thank you. I'm sorry for the trouble."

My saying this made a certain softness appear on her face. "No trouble at all," she said. "Just come right back to me when you know what you want to do."

I thanked her again, then on impulse said, "I have a sister named Stephanie," to which she smiled more than I'd thought she might.

"Well, tell her hello for me," she said. "We have to stick together." It made me feel happy, her saying that silly thing, and I told her I would. I turned and made the mistake of seeing some of the faces in line as they looked up from their phones—I had expected them to appear irritated, but instead I saw something else in them, pity or fear or fascination, I couldn't be sure which. Maybe all. Exiting the bank I felt genuinely calmer, not the false calm I'd earlier tried to persuade myself to feel. I drove a little faster toward home than I had leaving the therapist's office, less afraid now that I'd make a mistake.

Let him see that I have not cashed his bribe. Let him worry about what it means. Let him dread a phone call, an email, a new patient—a young man—arriving for his first appointment, sitting down in that chair to accuse him of being his dad.

Dad: how much I know Will longs to say that word. If the therapist isn't going to offer that, I'm not going to give my son the consolation prize this check represents.

Besides, what would it say about me if I accepted

money from a person who did what he did?

He'll be all right without it, he'll find a way to support himself and pay off his loans and earn a living, the same as I did. If worse comes to worst, Jack and Grettie will help him, until he can stand on his own two feet.

There's a reason I named you Will.

Thinking all this made my chest feel light. I gripped the steering wheel even tighter, so I wouldn't float away.

I'd thought that all I wanted to do was get home, change into comfy clothes, and lie down with my book; it was what I had been aiming toward all day. But before I reached my own street, I realized there was something I wanted—needed—to do first. Had it been brewing in my mind the whole time, and I'd just forgotten? It didn't seem so, but lately I wasn't a good judge.

I knew the address by heart, but I didn't know where the street was, so I pulled over to turn on the GPS. I was six miles from my destination, it said. The route looked straightforward, going on back roads. Ten minutes later I found it—where Celia Santoro lives.

It was a side street, so I could slow down in front of the house. The inside was dark, which I found disappointing. But of course—she was probably still at work, right? Most people still went to offices.

If she had returned to work, that is. I couldn't remember the date of her heart maze procedure. Maybe she was still recovering, taking a nap in her bedroom. Did she live alone with her little boy? It was a small enough house that she might have. If there had been information about this in her file, I'd forgotten it. I found myself hoping she had someone to take care of her—if not a partner, then at least a friend like the kind of friend Grettie has been to me.

Even if there had been lights on inside the house, it didn't mean I would catch a glimpse of her. For that is what I'd been hoping, I realized: I wanted to see this woman whose health I'd been tracking and coding all these years, whom I'd come to see as some kind of psychic twin. It was silly, I knew. I also knew that in allowing myself finally to take this trip, I'd lost that fantasy. Maybe that was my motivation—I recognized that the time had come, I'd reached the point at which I must give things up.

None of this was conscious, of course. But sometimes the unconscious things are the ones we know best. The therapist had told me that once and I believed him, though now I can't be sure what, if anything, he should have been trusted about.

But wait—here was a car pulling into the driveway of Celia's house. I could see even before it parked that it was a woman driving, with a child in the rear booster seat. Though the light was dim, I could make out his face at the window, absorbed in a daydream. This was the son she'd had six years ago; seeing him in person, rather than as a detail on my computer screen, gave me goosebumps. But it wasn't the kind of shivering I'd done in the therapist's office—this was a far better kind.

The driver had to be Celia, didn't it? I'd never seen a photograph, but it seemed to me I could make out that this woman's nose had undergone surgery, as I knew

Celia's had. As always with such things, she didn't look anything like what I had imagined. On another day this would have disappointed me, but I didn't have the energy for that now. Instead I allowed myself to think *There she is*, with the same pleasure I might have felt encountering Grettie or my sister when I hadn't expected it. Instead of the long, dark hair I had pictured, Celia's hung in a blunt blond cut. I'd assumed for some reason that she'd be short, like me, but this woman was tall and lithe, like volleyball players I'd known in college. She had a pale face, no blush or lipstick as far as I could tell.

But even without lipstick, it was easy to make out her smile. The boy in the booster seat behind her must have said something, because she turned to him and laughed and was still smiling when he unbuckled himself and they both got out of the car.

Now I smiled, too, because he was wearing a faded red tee-shirt with Santa Claus on the front, over a pair of polka-dotted pink shorts. This meant, no doubt, that his mother had allowed him to dress himself, which I wish I had done more of with Will. I'm ashamed to say that if he'd put on a shirt with Santa on it in June, I would have made him change. I would have told myself it was because I didn't want him to be mocked, and yes that would have been part of it, but it also would have been because I knew people would think he had some kind of crazy or negligent mother, to let him go out like that when the season was wrong.

Celia's son lugged his Batman backpack out of the car, first dragging it on the driveway, then hoist-swing-ing it up to his mother, who took the bag and slung it over her own shoulder as if it contained hardly any weight at all. The boy ran ahead to the house and waited, and Celia followed without rushing, holding the bag to her side like something precious. (I knew it was.) Then they both vanished inside the house.

Before turning toward home I sat for a few minutes, savoring what seeing Celia made me feel. Why had I sought her out, at last?

A few reasons, I realized. Because—despite what I was doing my best to believe—I was not okay, and I wanted to make sure she was. Because it didn't matter anymore in terms of my work, I'd never code her file again. Because I wanted to see for once beyond the code, to what it stood for.

Thank you, I whispered, though I was not sure to whom.

The boy's backpack reminded me that it was the end of the school year. Maybe even the last day. Almost a year ago, after the canceled commencement, Will received his diploma in the mail. I was so happy then, and hopeful, celebrating the anniversary of my surgery and Will's acceptance to the school he wanted. I was recovered, and he was almost launched. That was a phew, indeed—the biggest one of all.

But my circumstances are revised now. My access has been amended. In front of Celia Santoro's house I turned the car around and headed, finally, toward home. My heart felt full, and not in the bad way it has so often lately.

As I drove down my own street, I saw a woman running toward me from one of the houses, waving with both arms for me to stop. Shit! I didn't feel like stopping. All I wanted to do was get home and relax and read my book—was that too much to ask?

Well, I guess so, because here came this woman, trying to flag me down.

This was the runner, I realized. She ran the loop of the neighborhood in good weather and bad, never very fast but with a loping determination it was hard to ignore.

I myself had been a runner, as a young woman, but I stopped during my pregnancy and never resumed. I wouldn't have been able to explain my reasoning; it just struck me as unseemly, somehow, the idea of a mother running.

But: I had enjoyed it. Running used to calm me down, after Grettie finished her degree and moved to Boston, and before I followed her. I worked a support job in a doctor's office back then, sitting at a word processor and, as I listened through headphones I controlled with a pedal at my feet, entering onto the screen the notes my boss had dictated. Not every day, but when I could make myself, I got up early to run a loop of the neighborhood cemetery. I liked passing the graves, imagining from their names and the dates of their lifetimes what the people were like, wondering if they were at peace now, and what that might mean. When I got to that part of the route I turned the volume down on my Walkman, out of respect. I always slept better the nights after I'd run. I dreamed about people at work, or the curtains in my childhood bedroom, or about being pregnant. In my dreams, I gave birth to birds.

I considered pretending I hadn't seen the woman waving for me to stop. But then, I thought, it might be a real emergency ... The way she looked was the way I felt so often, including as recently as an hour ago in the therapist's office: desperate and panicked, wishing to be swooped in upon and saved. I pulled over and turned the engine off.

"Oh, thank you," she said, stretching forward with her hands on the car's hood in a child's pose while she caught her breath. "I need your help. My cat's on the roof again and I can't get him down by myself."

I breathed out more loudly than I'd intended. "That's all? The way you were running at me, I thought somebody was having a heart attack."

The woman said she was sorry. "It's just that I can't do it alone."

I considered telling her I wasn't in any condition, after the day I'd just been through, to help rescue a cat. But then I thought, what if I need help with Scout someday? So I decided to get out of the car. Though I passed this house every day on my way in or out of the neighborhood, I noticed only now the circular stained-glass window above the front door. Had it been there all along? Whether for a decade or a day, I was sure that I was seeing it now for the first time. Will told me once that most people don't notice most of what is around them, most of the time. From a psychology class he took in high school, he described an experiment in which subjects were asked to count the number of ball exchanges among a group of six people on a basketball court. During the action, the scientists conducting the experiment sent a person wearing a gorilla suit onto the court among the players. About half the test subjects reported never seeing the gorilla, so intent were they on their assigned task of counting how many times the ball got passed. "It's called intentional blindness," Will said. "A failure of awareness, because you're choosing to focus on something else."

We'd had this discussion during his birthday dinner the year he turned fourteen. When I told him I couldn't quite believe that so many people were that oblivious, he said, "Well, it's not really obliviousness, so much. It's missing details because you're not looking for them. The whole point is not just that you didn't notice, but that you have no idea you're not noticing."

He used "you" in this case to mean "everyone," and this I understood, but it was still hard not to feel that he was accusing me personally. I remember thinking that he was one of only two people remaining in the world with the power to hurt me. As it turns out, there are three.

When I stood at the side of my car, the woman took a step back. "Don't worry, I just spilled some garbage," I told her. "I'm going to take a shower as soon as I get home."

"It's not that." She looked scared, which made me regret having stopped to help her. "Should you even be driving? I don't really need help—listen, I changed my mind."

"What are you talking about? You pulled me over.

I'm here, let's do it." When she tried to put me off again I walked past her and started toward the backyard, where I saw a ladder set up against the eave. A black cat with a white spot on its throat craned to look down at both of us with (I felt it distinctly, though I am a dog person instead of a cat one) an air of amusement.

"My son used to say *heart attach* instead of *heart attack*," I told the woman, as she put a foot on the first rung. Then she put the foot back down and looked at me.

"I really think I should just wait for my husband," she said. "I'm sorry I bothered you—I didn't realize."

"Realize what?" I dared her to say it.

"I'm not sure you understand your situation," she told me, under her breath. "I can ask someone else. My husband should be home soon."

I was irritated by all of it—her speaking so low I almost couldn't hear her, her presuming I didn't know what was going on, her rubbing it in that she was married.

"Go ahead," I told her, gesturing at the ladder. "I don't have all the time in the world, I have to get back home."

When she saw that I wasn't going to give in, she started climbing reluctantly and sent down instructions from above. "If you hold it steady, I can go up to the top step. Then he knows to crawl onto on my back, and I lower us both down to the ground."

As she climbed, she said she'd never seen me before. She asked how long I'd lived in the neighborhood, and I told her eighteen years. Oh. Where had I lived before, then? I told her where I'd moved when I first came here, where I gave birth to Will. "Oh," the woman said, "that's more convenient in a lot of ways, but out here we have the peace and quiet."

That reminded me. Part of me wanted to ask and part of me didn't, and the part that wanted to won. "Hey, did you hear all those sirens earlier? What were those about?"

She had almost reached the ladder's top, but she stopped to peer down at me with a puzzled look. "What sirens? I didn't hear any sirens."

"How could you not hear them?"

I thought she might take offense at this, but instead she paused to consider. "I don't really pay attention unless it has something to do with me."

Well, when she said that, I was left to wonder whether there had been any sirens at all. Now that I thought about it, wouldn't I have heard something about it by now, if Derek Foote had followed through on his threat to do something big, something bad? In the line behind me at the bank, every person had been looking down at a phone. They weren't saying to each other, *Hey, did you see this*? And Celia Santoro, if that's who she was, had not appeared nervous or agitated. She had not hustled her son into the house.

It comforted me, the idea that I'd been wrong about the sirens. That I'd only thought I heard them, that it might have been just a symptom of the anxiety I felt as I drove to the therapist's. That wouldn't be so surprising, I realized. I'd been very anxious, after all.

The woman's shoulders were level with the roof now,

and the cat reached its nose out to sniff her sleeve. To change the subject I said, "So this is a thing, with the roof? Does he go up there a lot?"

"Only if something scares him—the wind, a big truck, another cat. But I didn't hear anything this time, I don't know what got into him."

The cat's name was Jasmine, the woman told me as we performed the rescue. Even though it was a male, her son had insisted that they give the new kitten the same name as the cat they were replacing. This worked out fine because they could just call him Jazz, the woman went on, as if it mattered or as if I cared.

She went on to say that the original Jasmine had died in a coyote attack in their backyard. "I had no idea they would be so bold as to come right onto our patio like that. But that was in winter. We figured it couldn't find any other food."

I did not tell her, as I was tempted to, that I often heard the wailing of coyotes—as recently as a few nights ago—and it was on the cusp of summertime now. I did not say that I considered the neighborhood's location near the woods, our proximity to the wild, the price we all pay for the peace and quiet we enjoy out here.

The sound those coyotes make together is terrible— an army advancing, wolves closing in for the kill.

"I cried more for that cat than I did when my father died." She sounded as if she hadn't realized it before. "I don't want to go through that again."

Well, there was not much I could say to this. Instead I told her that even though I'd never gone to church as a child, I always imagined getting married in a sanctuary with a stained-glass window like the one above her front door. "I pictured walking down the aisle at my wedding and seeing those beautiful colors lit up by the sun. I thought it would be the most perfect moment of my life."

"Yeah, that's what we all thought," the woman said. She laughed and waited for me to join her, and when I didn't, she stopped as if she were ashamed, as if she'd just let out a fart or something.

Finally the new Jasmine climbed onto her back, and the woman lowered herself and the cat slowly to the ground. After she nudged him inside the sliding glass door, we exchanged emails and phone numbers. Her email address included the word *Happymom.* For God's sake, I thought. Only a few minutes later would I realize that though I now had enough information to contact her, I still did not know her name.

To make conversation as she walked me back to my car, I asked her what she thought about Arcadia Glen. "Oh, it's wrong what they're doing," she said. "Don't you think?"

By *they,* she could have meant the developer and the people who wanted to move the old cemetery, or she could have meant the people who were trying to stop them. Of course I could not answer her question without knowing which, but I didn't ask. Instead I just made the same murmur I've rehearsed to perfection over the years, not committing to anything.

In front of her house, my car started as soon as I turned the key—something to be glad for. "I wish you could stay longer," the woman said, and I was sure I must be mistaken to think I detected grief in her eyes. But then it was in her voice, too. "I'm sorry you have to go."

"That was weird," I said out loud as I pulled away. I watched her recede in my mirror as she watched after me and hugged herself, as if in spite of how hot it was, a sudden chill had seized her.

It was probably not even five-thirty when I got home, considering that the meeting with the therapist had taken less time than a regular session; the route from his office to my house was a reverse commute at that hour; I was first in line at the bank; I'd done a mere drive-by past Celia's; and the encounter with *Happymom*, though it felt longer, lasted only about fifteen minutes.

As I was making my way up to my front door, Pascal emerged from her own. She came closer than I expected her to, closer than I would have liked. "Oh, God, Roberta," she said, taking one of my elbows. "Let me help you."

But I shook her off. "I can do it," I told her. "I'm not dead yet!" At the laugh I gave to accompany these words, she looked stricken, but backed off and hurried into her house.

When I got inside I went straight into the bathroom to pee, realizing only then that I'd had to do so since I woke up from my nap in the therapist's parking lot. But nothing came out. I haven't been drinking enough, I thought. I should have had more water today, not coffee, not Diet Coke. I went into the kitchen, filled up a big glass, and tried to drink it down all at once. But my throat wouldn't let me, it seemed to close up. I stood at the counter and took little sips instead. I still felt thirsty, but I managed to produce a little pee.

Before I flushed, I ripped the therapist's check into tiny pieces and dropped them into the bowl. So what if I mucked up the plumbing–what I felt, watching those bits spin and vanish, was worth it.

I thought about turning on the TV as I usually did, for the company of voices. Then I decided not to, thinking it would be nice to have some peace and quiet.

Who am I kidding? Just in case Derek had done something, I didn't want to hear the news.

I should take a shower, I knew. I smelled, probably worse than before. I managed to twist my tee-shirt off over my head, but for a minute I couldn't think of what was supposed to come next. I went into my bedroom and slipped into a sweatshirt from Will's college. I love this sweatshirt, it's soft, it makes me think of him. I might not wear anything besides this, ever again.

Scout was waiting for me, waiting for his dinner. I poured food into his bowl, unable to keep it from spilling over the sides, then sat down at the kitchen table. Instead of going to eat right away, he came over to tilt his head up at me and put his chin on my knee.

Oh, Scout, you're such a good boy. It's going to be so hard to lose you when the time comes.

I went out to the screened porch, lay down on the chaise and pulled the comforter over my legs, then over my arms when I couldn't get warm. I rested awhile, then picked up my novel. It opened to the part about Clarissa's kiss from Sally. *The whole world might have turned upside down! The others disappeared ... And she felt that she had been given a present, wrapped up, and told just to keep it, not to look at it—a diamond, something infinitely precious... the radiance burnt through, the revelation, the religious feeling!*

I closed my eyes thinking I might drown in it, what flooded me as I read. I guess it overcame me, because I fell asleep. When I woke up I didn't want to move from where I was, but I had to go to the bathroom again. Resenting my body for the power it had over me, I pushed the comforter aside and lifted myself up, then made my way from the porch to the living room, where I saw Derek Foote sitting on the couch.

"What! *You're* here?" To my surprise, I did not feel shocked or scared—just a little annoyed. Only a few hours ago he'd promised me he'd stop doing this, breaking into people's houses. Did I mean so little to him—was my threat to call the police such an obviously empty one—that he could be so brazen in ignoring it, and me?

He held a hand up as if to defend himself from what he knew I must be thinking. "I didn't break in, I promise. You left the door unlocked."

"No. I wouldn't have done that." Yet now that I said it, did I actually remember securing the latch with my key after rushing home to change clothes between the dump and the therapist's office? I did not. But then, I've been forgetting a lot of things lately.

"You did, though." Derek's tone was not mocking, not accusatory, but gentle. "I was relieved, to be honest. I would have felt bad about breaking into your house. I don't know if I could have brought myself to do it. But I wanted to make sure you were okay."

Well, I could have said what we all say, in this kind of conversation. It would have been easy to utter the words—*I'm fine*—but I understood that we were beyond the point at which either of us would believe it, now. I also understood that Derek had not actually been asking the question, or deluding himself that he might find me in better shape than when he'd seen me last. What he was really saying was *I like you, I'm sorry this is happening, I came here to be with you.* I felt grateful to him for it, but for some reason I couldn't manage to tell him so.

"I also wanted to make sure you heard what I said today." He sat calmly, eating from a bag of pretzels I'd bought a long time ago for when Will came home, but never opened. Was Derek calm? I couldn't really tell, but if not, he fooled me. He hadn't turned on the TV, as he did in other people's houses—in deference, I supposed, to the fact that he'd found me sleeping when he came in. "I wanted to make sure you wouldn't forget what I told you, that I wished you were my mother instead of her." He pointed a pretzel in the direction of Grettie's neighborhood and his own house, where his mother was no doubt still hoping to get him into a program that would redirect him and teach him a half-smile.

"I didn't forget it," I told him. "I thought it was very nice. I was glad you said that—it meant a lot to me."

"It's true," he said, crunching. "Anybody who doesn't get how lucky he is to have you for a mother is completely insane."

Well, now he was talking about Will, and I couldn't let him get away with that. But neither could I think of exactly how to respond. I sat down on the couch, leaving a cushion between us. Scout was lying at my feet, making little whimpers. Some watchdog! But we hadn't gotten him to be a watchdog. We got him for the love.

"Something else I wanted to say." Derek hung his head, looking guilty. "I let you believe something that isn't true. I know what you were thinking earlier, when you caught me in the house. It wasn't Will who called in that bomb threat at graduation. It was me."

God bless him! "Thank you for telling me that," I said. I hoped he knew how much I appreciated it, even though I couldn't muster what it would take to believe him.

Having listened to all that came before this, you can imagine how I felt—what my heart did—when the front door opened and I heard my son step inside to look for me, calling out, "Mom? I'm home." For a moment I felt confused, thinking that it was not Will as he is now, but the Will he'd been as a little boy. Instinctively I pushed my sleeve up, knowing as he approached that when he bent down to greet me he would give me a kiss on the forehead and then reach out to rub my arm. *Heart maze. Heart attach. Look what I can do!*

"You came," I said, though this was obvious, it was a waste of breath I could have saved myself. "Why?"

"Grettie called me. She'll be here soon." He gave a bitter laugh, but no, that's not what it was. It was a blast of something else—panic. What had she told him? And where was she?

"But how did you get here so fast?"

"Oh, please, don't worry about that," Will said, try-ing to wave my question away. "It doesn't matter, does it?" When I told him that Yes, it did matter to me, he sighed and I watched him struggle to figure out how to respond. "I wasn't as far away as I told you. I'm sorry about that, Mom. I was still mad at you. We've been clos-er than you thought."

We. Had he brought Sosi with him? I didn't see her, but that didn't mean she wasn't there. I was about to ask when he pointed at Derek and said, "Why the fuck are *you* here?"

Derek raised a hand, the one not holding the pret-zels, against what sounded like an accusation from his old friend. "Extenuating circumstances," he said quiet-ly. I was impressed by that—it was a good way to put it, I thought, a good way to describe what was happening now. I took over the best I could, clarifying for Will about Derek and the break-ins. How they were harmless. How Derek was just looking for a place to get away from his mother and have a nonapproved snack. How this time, in our house, he hadn't actually broken in.

Will seemed to accept both our explanations. But then he said, "I still don't see why he needs to be here. Considering—" but he didn't need to finish the sentence, we all knew what he was talking about.

"Your mom saved me," Derek told him. His voice contained a measure of wonder. "There was something big I was going to do, something bad, that she talked me out of." The expression on his face suggested that he felt startled by this turn of events, as if he himself had not been responsible for the better decision he'd ended up making.

"Oh, I'm so glad!" I hoped he heard the exclamation point I was trying to convey. It relieved me more than I would have expected, to know he hadn't gone through with his crazy plan. I told him, "I'm proud of you."

Will dropped to his knees between me and Derek, next to where I half-sat, half-lay on the sofa. "Why didn't you tell me you were sick again?" I don't think I'd ever heard his voice as anguished as he sounded then, even during the worst of his emetophobia. It cracked something awful, like when he was thirteen.

"Well, at first, I didn't think it was that bad," I told him. "I kept thinking the treatments might work. And I didn't want to disrupt you at school."

"But when you found out it was that bad?" He pressed his temples hard with the heels of his hands. "I could have taken a leave of absence or something. If I'd known, I would never have stayed away—God, I could just kick myself!"

"Oh, honey, don't say that." But I'd made a mistake; I'd heard *kill myself.* Then I remembered this wasn't like him, I was the one who'd thought about doing that. "I didn't want you to take a leave of absence. I didn't want you to come home unless you wanted to." I had a clear mind about this, and it felt good to be able to say what I meant. "And you didn't want to."

He took a long, deep breath, and I assumed he was picturing narrow streams of air moving in and out of his nostrils, the way he'd learned in tai chi. *Don't fight it and it will be easier.* "I'm sorry," he said again, sounding more like himself this time, and I smiled to let him know it was okay, even though it wasn't.

Derek said to Will, "Your mom and I were just talking about that bomb threat at graduation. How it was me who called it in, and how I shouldn't have done it."

I tried not to notice as Will flushed, took a quick breath, and looked away. Beyond the grudging gratitude his eyes threw toward Derek, I recognized another expression on his face. "It's come back, honey?" I asked, remembering only then what he had told me on the phone at Christmas. "The trouble with your tummy?"

"A little bit, sometimes." He reached over to touch my hand. "But don't worry, it'll get better. Hey, guess what, I decided to take your advice. When I start to feel sick, I say to myself, I am just a biological organism; this anxiety is coming from a thought I can control; there is not really anything to be afraid of."

"Oh, I'm so glad that works." It had failed for me when I tried it, but he was a different person, I was glad if I'd suggested something that helped. "Listen, I've been wondering something. The speech you were going to give at commencement—what was it about?"

Another sharp breath in, and a further blush. "Well, it was about you. Are you surprised? Of course it was. How you helped me so much with everything, how I couldn't have done it without you." Now he folded my hand inside his own. He held on too tight, but of course I didn't say so. "I'll read it to you someday, just not right now, okay?"

I said "Okay" and tried to lift my head. It made me feel dizzy, but I didn't mind, after what he'd just said. "You didn't have to write a speech," I told him. "I would have been happy just to see you walk across the stage and pick up your diploma. Hear them call your name." I did my best impression of a deep announcer's voice. "*Will Chase.*"

What will you chase, Will? You will chase what?

The three of us just sat there then, like a little family. There was a change in the air, it was as if we all understood something without it needing to be said. As if we'd all agreed not to waste any more time talking about things we should or should not have done. Will seemed not to mind anymore that Derek was there—or if he did, he didn't show it. We reminisced, if you could call it that. Or the boys did, I just listened. They talked about the pancakes, the ones I made after sleepovers. About Lego ships, the cartoons. More than once, with my eyes closed, I thought I heard them laugh, the most perfect sound in the world. The way a singer's voice can break glass at a high pitch, it split me in half. *Phew,* I remember thinking. I might even have said it out loud. "That was a phew."

"A few what?" Derek asked. He leaned in to hear me better, but it was Will who explained it to him. Your piece is in the last row of Chutes and Ladders and you're trying to get to the end, you can see ahead to the blue ribbon, but two or three or four spaces in front of you is the square that will plunge you all the way back down to the beginning. You want to avoid that number. But you have no control over it—you just hold your breath and spin.

Will said he'd always hated that game: it was too stressful.

"I liked it." Derek pointed at his chest to claim the opposite. "I used to play that game all the time."

Then I heard Grettie whispering to someone. Grettie! What was this? When had she arrived? There were other voices on the screened porch, it sounded like a party but without the cheer. Pascal appeared, then crossed the room to switch the lamp on. "Don't worry," she told Will, putting a hand on his shoulder. "I called them."

Called who? I wondered. I had not seen her come in, but things were a little shadowy, it was possible I'd missed it. Pascal had not been in my house for years, but she still seemed to know where everything was. It felt familiar to have her here, now. More than familiar—it felt good.

"I'm sorry for the trouble between us," I told her. "All those years lost, over such a silly thing."

"It wasn't a silly thing." Her smile was kind, though, and I could see it was not her intention to argue. "But I'm sorry, too." She moved out of the light again.

For a moment, I thought I might be hallucinating all these people in my house, the exact ones I would have invited at a time like this.

But no, my sister wasn't here. That's how I knew it was all real—I would have conjured her if I could. Turning to the window, I saw that it had gotten dark outside on the longest day of the year, which meant that a number of hours had passed, maybe three or more, since I returned from seeing the therapist. Enough time for all of these people to gather for my extenuating circumstance.

I might have dozed for a while, then. I might have dreamed. It was like a movie with a soundtrack: *O Holy Night, the stars are brightly shining.* In the dream I finally told Grettie the truth about my pregnancy, and asked if she would pass the information on to Will when she thought he could handle it. Not now, but someday—when he was out of school and on his way in the world, when the emetophobia was a mere speck in his rearview mirror.

When he hadn't just lost me.

"Of course I'll tell him," Grettie said. "But are you sure you don't want to do it yourself, before you—go?"

That was how I knew it was a dream, or whatever you want to call it. In real life, if I'd told her what I just had about the therapist, she would have said, "That fucker! I'll make him pay."

The answer I'd have given her was that I'll protect Will as long as I can, from what I know has the power to hurt him. I hope it's forever. Even if he does find out whose son he is, there'll be no one to tell him the real circumstances of how he came to be.

It's better this way, right? He won't know the truth, but what will the truth matter, then?

I can stand the pain of this. I can stand it. The only thing I want is to know if he'll forgive me, for all the ways I failed.

"Yes," Sosi said, nodding, "he will." Then I thought she added, "Whether you deserve it or not," but I might be wrong about that, that might not have been what I heard.

She sat next to Will on the loveseat, her arm pressing into his thigh. I said, "Oh, hi, Sosh," and I could tell that my voice was not warm—I couldn't help it. Though it's only fair for me to admit that I'm glad he has her, especially now. "I didn't see you there."

She had the oddest sense of being herself invisible, unseen; unknown ...

It was time to do more than murmur, no point in codes anymore. Grettie helped me sit myself up on one elbow to find some extra breath and I said "I love you"— to Will, and to her.

Who am I kidding, I said it to them all. And, now a surprise: I said it not just to the people in the room, but to all the others outside it, too. The awful tennis coach, the pretend yoga teacher, the nurses in their parrot shirts, my friends at work. The old lady in the hospital lobby singing her old, indecipherable song. Celia and her son in his Santa shirt. The people at the dump who'd yelled at me, the Arcadia Glen developer, the neighbors who hated him, and Trudy Foote with her bags of poop. My sister and the bank teller who had the same name. *Happymom.*

Even the therapist—because I had loved him once, before that day a long time ago, and without him, I wouldn't have Will.

This was my life and the people in it. The world I had to leave before I was ready, before I wanted to. Why not say I loved them? It couldn't hurt anything, it could only help.

My son's face twisted. It was the face he used to make when he was afraid he was on the verge of being sick. "Mom, *please*."

Oh! What did he mean by that? Was he asking the central question of his life one last time, thinking I was finally in no position to deny him? Or was it the beginning of an apology, because he knew he'd asked the question too many times?

Or was he begging me not to die? Mom, *please*. It made my chest hurt, having to wonder.

And being unsure if it was a question, I couldn't risk saying anything that might sound like an answer. Instead of giving him a response I lay back on the cushion, because that was the easiest thing.

Grettie's lips trembled. She reached down to hug me, so I wasn't cold anymore. I heard a siren in the distance—or was it closer than it seemed?

Everything after that I don't remember. But it doesn't matter, because this is the end.

Acknowledgments

For the generous gift of their time, editorial comments, encouragement, and expertise about certain details, I am indebted to Ann Treadway, Molly Johnson, Laura Gergel (earliest readers from the earliest days), Katie Gergel, Jean Lucey, Karen Feldscher, Lauren Richman, Adam Schwartz, Lisa Breger, Julia Glass, Elisa Bronfman, Christine Primiano, and Pam Warren-Brooks. For their continuing support on behalf of my work, heartfelt appreciation to Kimberly Witherspoon, Jessica Mileo, William Callahan and the rest of the team at Inkwell, as well as my friends and colleagues at Emerson College. For publication, production, and promotion, my deep gratitude to the Delphinium crew of Lori, Joe, and Colin. And as ever my love and thanks to Philip Holland for all he does and gives to me, which is more than he knows.

About the Author

Jessica Treadway is the Flannery O'Connor Award–winning author of the story collections *Please Come Back to Me* and *Absent Without Leave* (Delphinium Books), and the novels *And Give You Peace*, *Lacy Eye*, and *How Will I Know You?* She is a Senior Distinguished Writer in Residence at Emerson College in Boston.